ARKADY

Patrick Langley is a writer who lives in London. He writes about art for *frieze*, *Art Agenda*, and other publications. He is a contributing editor at *The White Review*. *Arkady* is his first novel.

'Patrick Langley's *Arkady* is a strange trip — luminescent, jagged and beautiful. A debut novel that twists, compels, descends and soars. I highly recommend it.'
— Jenni Fagan, author of *The Panopticon*

'*Arkady* is a utopian project: not the top-down kind that never works, but the bottom-up kind that (in this case anyway) works so well it reclaims something of the world. It's hand-built, beautifully, from loose memories, salvaged people, and wild blooms of the psychogeographical sublime. Tense, vivid and humane, this novel gives us not only a dark future but also – over the horizon, past the next riverbend, through that hole in the fence – a chance of saving ourselves from it.'
— Ned Beauman, author of *Boxer, Beetle*

'Langley's invented metropolis was a joy to spend time in. In my visual imagination, it looked as if it had been half-painted by L. S. Lowry and finished off by H. R. Giger. And the ambience was a little bit *Stalker*, and a little bit *Tekkonkinkreet*. But then at the heart of it all was this complex, tender relationship between brothers, and Langley's writing – which somehow managed to be both unembellished and evocative.'
— Sara Baume, author of *A Line Made by Walking*

'The Romulus and Remus of a refugee nation embark upon a drift across livid cities, liberatory canals and compromised occupations in a parallel present mere millimetres from our own. Langley gives to the reader the taste of the Molotov fumes and the bloody heft of the personal-political in this propulsive, acid fable, a *dérive* for the age of urbex. How can the orphaned subject escape the surveillance state? Read on to find out. We, also, are in Arcadia.'
— Mark Blacklock, author of *I'm Jack*

Fitzcarraldo Editions

ARKADY

PATRICK LANGLEY

CONTENTS

I. ANOTHER COUNTRY

A fan stirs the room's thick heat as the officers talk. Jackson wags his legs under the chair and watches his shoes as they swing. The officers speak about beaches. A pathway. Red flags. The story does not make sense. When they finish it, Jackson looks up. The door is open. It frames a stretch of shrivelled lawn and a column of cloudless sky. Colours throb in the heat.

'Do you understand?' the woman asks.

'We are sorry,' says the man.

Blue uniforms cling to their arms. Black caps are perched on their heads. Jackson peers into the caps' plastic rims, which slide with vague shadows and smears of light. The officers mutter to each other and swap glances with hooded eyes. The breeze through the door is like dog-breath, a damp heat that smells faintly of rot.

'Where's my dad?' asks Jackson.

The man's thumb is hooked through his belt. He stands like a cowboy, hips cocked.

'We don't know,' he sighs. 'Our colleague saw him a moment after. We're sure he'll come back soon. You have a small brother? We take you to the place, and you tell him. Tell him your father is coming back. We'll find him. I promise. Right now.'

They are staying on the side of a mountain, a short but twisting drive away from the nearest coastal town. The hotel is enormous. From a distance it resembles a castle, its high walls strong and stern, its red roofs bright against the mountain's grey. The valley below is dotted with scrubby bushes and half-finished breezeblock homes. At its centre, a dried-up riverbed runs through copses of stunted trees: a jagged path connecting the hotel to the town.

Frank is in the crèche with the other toddlers. They

crawl and stumble on the floor, slapping primary-coloured mats with chubby palms. Jackson glances at the sprinkler outside. Threads of water glitter like glass until they shatter and fall. He asks the woman when the children go home.

'When does the session finish, you mean?' she asks. She is English. Her eyes are the dull blue of cloudless skies. 'Is everything alright?'

Jackson's brother is in the far corner, a monkey teddy in his hand. He is wearing his robot pyjamas; his smile makes Jackson smile.

'You can come back at five o'clock, if you like,' the woman says. 'We have a painting class. Do you like art? You could do a jigsaw?'

Frank smacks a beat on the monkey-doll's stomach. Thump-thump!

'The one in the corner,' says Jackson.

'You know him?'

'He's my brother.'

The woman smiles at Jackson, briefly narrowing her eyes. 'He's very good,' she says.

The swimming pool is white and blue. It hurts Jackson's eyes to look at it. In the evenings, before dinner, his mother will swim for a while and then relax on a lounger, sunglasses masking her eyes, and read a book while their father plays tennis, goes walking, or naps. Today a strange woman has taken his mother's lounger. Her legs are bronzed and dimpled, with blue worms squiggling under the skin. Her lips are the colour of cocktail cherries, sticky and red.

'You alright there pal?'

The man is on a lounger. Gold things shine at his knuckles and neck: he is either a king or a thief.

'Here on your own?' The man is from Jackson's city. That voice. 'Where are your parents?' He is wearing skimpy Y-front trunks, the kind Jackson's mother calls budgie smugglers. His tanned skin shines like oiled meat. 'You speak English? *Española*? Where are your *parentés*, your *grandays persona*? Big people, you know?' He chuckles. 'Mum? Dad? Parents? No?'

A waiter appears with a tray. On his tray is a bright blue drink in a tall glass shaped like a space rocket. A wedge of pineapple, skewered on a toothpick, glistens in the sun. The woman places her hand on her heart and – 'Ah!' – her teeth flash as she gasps.

'My man,' says the man on the lounger, clicking his fingers. 'Over here.'

The woman slips the fruit into her mouth.

'Of course,' says the waiter, smiling. The red splodge on the pocket of his shirt is the hotel's logo: a mermaid sitting sadly on a rock. 'Another beer, sir?'

Everyone smiles.

The budgie-smuggler shakes his head. 'This boy,' he says, 'he's been standing there for the last five minutes. Hasn't said a thing.'

'I see,' the waiter says.

A crucifix hangs at the waiter's neck. His nose is long and straight, like a statue's. He is tall and strong and has very white teeth but his eyes are too close together. 'Hey lil' man,' he says, walking over, smiling so wide the creases reach his ears. 'You looking for your mother? You want me to try and call her?'

Jackson squints. Sweat pours down his forehead and stings his eyes. 'She doesn't have a phone,' he says. 'People call her all the time and she hates it. I went to tell Frank, but he's playing with a monkey.'

The waiter frowns and sticks his lower lip out. 'There's

no monkeys here.'

Jackson explains about the crèche.

'Ahhhhh, *sea sea sea* – your baby brother! I remember now.' Spanish people love the sea, they say it all the time. 'Well, let me think.' The waiter taps his chin with a finger. 'Ah, I saw your father this morning. He bought a snorkel from Reception.'

Jackson nods. 'That was before.'

When the waiter squats beside him, the muscles on his lower legs bulge. He smells of lemon peel, soap, and sweat.

'Why don't you come with me,' the waiter says. 'We're gonna do a search. I'm sure she's not far.'

Jackson rests his elbows on the marble bar. He worries the rim of an electric-blue beer mat until the cardboard frays to powder. The room has the feel of a mountain cave: cool, dim, secluded, and quiet. The only other people are an ancient couple with crepe paper faces, baggy earlobes, beige-and-white clothing and shapeless velcro shoes. They sip white wine and stare at nothing. Ferns with sword-like leaves stand guard at the circular tables.

'Detective work is hard,' the waiter says. 'You wanna eat something? Drink something? On the house.'

'Whose house?'

'My house,' the waiter says. 'You never heard that before?' He gestures at the windows, the room, the bar.

'It's a hotel.'

The waiter grins and wags a finger at Jackson. 'Very good,' he chuckles. 'Very good!'

The high glass shelves are lined with bottled spirits, clear, brown, red and green liquids doubled by the mirror behind them. Jackson stares at his reflection. His freckle-dusted skin is tinged with red. His hair is so blond it looks white. He imagines it isn't a mirror but a window into a separate room in which another young boy is sitting. The waiter hands Jackson a narrow glass crammed with ice and coke. Bubbles prickle his nose as he drinks.

'Good?' the waiter smiles.

Jackson nods. The ice hurts his teeth but he doesn't stop drinking. Soon he has drained the whole glass.

'Don't worry,' the waiter says, lifting a wall-mounted phone to his ear. 'We're gonna find her. I call my father now. This whole hotel – he owns it. Big man,' the waiter says, puffing his chest out, 'sitting in his big office, like this.' Jackson laughs. 'He will know. He knows everything.'

'Everything?'

'Well,' the waiter says, 'not *everything*. He's not God.' He rolls his eyes in a silly way. Jackson catches sight of himself in the mirror. He hisses and bares his teeth.

The waiter talks in Spanish on the phone. Jackson turns the glass on its side. A cube of ice slides across the marble in a puddle of melt. He places the cube in his mouth and presses it against the inside of his cheek with his tongue.

The waiter scrunches up his face. '*Qué?*'

Jackson listens to the voice at the other end of the line. Not the words, which he can't understand, but the noise they make, a raspy buzz. It sounds as though a wasp is trapped in the handle, trying to get out. The ice cube burns the skin of his mouth and the meltwater pools in his gums.

'*Qué?*' the waiter says, louder.

The trapped wasp screams and falls suddenly quiet. The room feels different, as though the temperature has dropped, or the furniture has rearranged itself around him. Open-mouthed, the waiter stares at Jackson, phone loose in his hand. It buzzes again: he ignores it. He sways a little on his feet, as though hit by a gust of wind.

'*Hostia*,' he says.

At dusk, the woman from the crèche sets up a camp bed in the brothers' room. Her name is Melissa. Earlier today, she spoke to Jackson in a laughing, sing-song voice; tonight, she seems wary of him. She shoots frequent, worried glances in his direction when she thinks he isn't looking. He catches her gaze for the hundredth time and scowls.

'Are you... okay?' she asks. 'Can I get you anything?'

Jackson is on his bed, legs bent, hugging his shins. 'Why do people keep asking me that?' The afternoon has been a blur of faces, bodies, rooms. Strangers materialise out of nowhere, shuffle him from place to place, and ask him how he is, how he's feeling, what he needs. Melissa looks surprised. 'Because they want to help you,' she says.

She peels off Frank's nappy and lowers him into the bath. Jackson watches from the doorway as she scoops the clouded water over Frank's shoulders, legs, and head. She uses less soap than their mother and does not sing. Jackson wants to tell her to stop, she's doing it wrong, his mother will do it. But he says nothing.

A soft knock on the door: a tray is ushered in, from room service. Melissa places it on the bed in front of Jackson. She tells him to eat. Instead, he watches the cheese on the cheeseburger stiffen and cool to yellow plastic. He pushes the plate to one side and lies face down on the duvet, eyes open, not moving his limbs.

'How about we play a game?' Melissa asks.

Jackson does not reply.

'TV, then. Say if you want it off.'

There are fields and rivers, butterflies and vines. A man in a baby-blue shirt and a funny hat stands by a waterfall, talking of networks of life. Jackson watches the shapes and colours move. His body feels hollow, like an emptied glass. Tilting his head, he looks outside. Molten orange and smoky purple stain the sky. The crickets have begun to sing. They fill the valley with clicks and whirrs, a chorus of tiny machines.

'Is he back yet?' he asks.

Melissa is sitting on the floor with her back to the bed, picking at a salad with her fork. She turns off the TV and places her hand on Jackson's shoulder.

'He'll be back soon,' she says.

Later, once the lights are out, stars appear in scattered patterns above the valley. Frank sprawls in his cot like a starfish, legs and arms pointing in different directions. His skin is as pale as dough. Melissa's bed creaks every time she moves. She makes a tent of the duvet and stares at her phone, buttons clicking as she types, the screen's halo pale on her face and hair.

Jackson shuts his eyes. He wishes he could press a button to make himself sleep. Instead he twists and turns in the sheet, wrapping his body up tight like a mummy until he can barely breathe. There is noise beyond the window, not just the crickets but the sound of the mountains, the roads, the sea. It sounds like people whispering. It sounds like somewhere else.

He wakes at the creak of the opening door. It feels as though no time has passed but he knows he must have slept because the light in the room has changed. Melissa is asleep. Tentacles of brown hair crawl across her pillow. Frank is sleeping too, his pink mouth slightly open, like a flower-bud.

Jackson's dad is in the doorway, blocking out the light. His presence sends a jolt through Jackson's body, a shudder of fear and relief.

'Who are you?' his father asks. His voice sounds crackly and thin, as though a radio is trapped in his throat.

He has not changed since Jackson last saw him, early this morning. His swimming trunks are yellowed with dust, his polo shirt is dark with sweat, and his sandals look scuffed on his sunburnt feet.

Melissa twists in her creaking bed and glances sleepily at the door. Jackson's dad tells her to leave. She gathers her stuff in her arms, an awkward bundle of phone, clothes, toothbrush and skin cream, and slopes into the corridor, head lowered like a scolded dog. The door clicks shut behind her. She doesn't say goodbye.

Jackson's father stands beside the camp bed, his face blank. He looks like a mannequin: lifeless, immobile, eyes empty and dull. Jackson grips the sheet so tight his knuckles ache. The air tastes thin and metallic as it slides into his lungs. His dad sits heavily on the bed. Wrists on his knees, head bowed, he stares unblinking at a patch on the floor. His mouth is slightly open. He stinks of sweat, of sea, of himself. Jackson desperately wants him to talk, to say something, anything – to tell him that policemen are liars – to laugh – to scruff his hair. Instead, he wraps Jackson up in his arms and holds him so close Jackson's ribs hurt. Damp breath roars in Jackson's ear. His arms go limp, his body numb. He stares at the ceiling, about to cry, but the tears don't come. His father rocks back and forth. The crickets' screaming begins to fade. Light grows stronger on the curtains: luminous blue.

Jackson spasms and kicks the cover, which clings to his clammy thighs. He must have fallen asleep again. The crickets have fallen silent. The room hums with yellowish light. Through the windows he sees low mountains, which shimmer on the valley's far side. Sunlight pours like honey down the crags.

'Dad,' says Jackson, rubbing his sleep-crusted eyes. 'Are you awake?'

His dad summons a long, gruff noise in his barrel chest: *hmmmmmmmh*. Normally his father is tall and solid, like a tree. Now he is a worm, limply draped across the floor.

'What happened? Where's Mum? Why are you on the floor?'

His dad inhales sharply but doesn't answer.

Frank chucks the monkey at the bars of his cot. He lifts his fat wrist to his mouth and sucks it with a thoughtful expression. He cries out, panicked, then smiles a heartbeat later. Sitting with his back to the headboard, Jackson bites his knee. He forces his front teeth down until it feels like the skin will rupture, and blood will gush into his mouth.

His dad staggers to Frank's crib. His eyes are sunken in their sockets, ringed with dark: he doesn't appear to have slept. In his hand is something wadded and white. It isn't a napkin or a tissue but their mother's linen shirt, crumpled up and jewelled with sand.

Slowly, as though underwater, his dad leans into the crib. Frank squirms. He whines and mewls as his dad lifts him, patting him on the back. Frank doesn't like it. He squirms even worse.

'Put your arms through his legs,' says Jackson. 'You're doing it wrong.'

His dad doesn't seem to have heard. He paces circles

in the room, singing snatched fragments and jostling his son. Frank's pyjamas shift as he wriggles and kicks: soon he will slip and fall.

Jackson rushes forward just in time. He grabs his brother in both arms, cradling his weight, and lowers Frank to the carpet: he looks up at Jackson and howls.

The police return later that morning. They ask for Jackson's father, who does not want to talk. He grits his teeth and rambles wildly, his crisped hair standing on end. The police persuade him down the corridor and into the lobby. Families mingle in swimming trunks and jazzy towels, straw hats and strappy vests. Some drag cases on screeching wheels. Others jab each other with pool-noodles, laughing as they parry and stab.

Jackson's dad prowls amongst them, yelling at people and walls. The officers ask him to *please calm down.* 'I will not fucking calm down.' He keeps saying it, over and over, putting the swear-word in different places each time. 'I will fucking not calm down. You haven't *found* her – you haven't fucking *found* her.'

Jackson knew it. She's playing a game, like hide and seek.

He ducks behind a fern, watching people through the mesh of leaves.

The waiter from yesterday raises his hands. 'Calm down, sir,' he says. 'Please. You are causing a scene.'

People in chino shorts and see-through dresses have begun to halt and gawp. Breakfast is almost over: a steady stream of people dawdle out of the restaurant's doors. The receptionist holds a phone halfway between the desk and her ear, mouth open, staring at Jackson's dad. Closest to him is a pair of women at a low glass table, sipping lemonade. Their enormous sunglasses, lurid yellow blouses and black bumbags make them look like oversized, wrinkly bumblebees.

'Sir, please,' the waiter says, reaching out to touch his shoulder, 'if we could—'

He moves one way and Jackson's dad moves the other. There's a muddle of limbs, an impulsive shove – the waiter loses balance. With flapping, wide-flung arms he topples onto the table, which crashes beneath his weight. Drinks glasses backflip, shed their liquid, and explode on the floor. The women leap and scream, neck-skin wagging as they howl. Reeling, drenched in lemonade, they gasp at Jackson's dad.

On the floor, the waiter winces. He looks like he's wet himself, the puddle pooled around his waist. Standing up, face twisted, he plucks something out of his palm. It flashes like a diamond in the sun. Red blood slithers down his wrist.

'Shit – listen – I didn't mean to do that,' says Jackson's dad.

Prickles chase each other over Jackson's skin. Something is wrong with the air-conditioning: the room is fridge-cold.

A policeman nods at the door and asks Jackson's dad to step inside.

'No,' says Jackson's dad.

'Sir,' the policeman says. 'Please.'

Stars go fizzing through the air, specks of light that swim and pulse through Jackson's eyes. He grips the side of the potted palm: the floor's tiles rock like waves. The clock behind the desk says 9 and he holds his breath. Holds it. His dad follows the policeman, dragging his heels. The door clicks shut. The receptionist, smiling, lifts the phone to her ear. Jackson slides to the floor and exhales.

Frank is on the bedroom floor, his plump legs folded, T-shirt bunched at his waist. Jackson stands above him for a moment, watching his brother play.

'Are you ready?' he eventually asks.

Frank claps and hiccups: 'Guh!'

The duffel bag, made from shiny blue fabric, has lots of pouches and zips. It bulges with their father's clothes, which he angrily stuffed into it on the morning of their flight: polo shirts, blue shorts, chino trousers, a pocket phrase book and a fold-out map. Jackson undoes the wide zip in the top of the duffel and empties half the contents. After folding the clothes in a pile on the floor, he stuffs a hotel towel and a few of his father's polo shirts: the end with the black plastic wheels. At the other end is a plastic handle.

Frank sucks at the skin of his wrist. Drool slicks down his forearm.

'In,' says Jackson, nodding. 'You go there. Sit still.'

He lifts Frank into the duffel and packs the towels and shirts around his waist to form a throne. Frank sits upright, legs crossed, and grips a towel's white corner. He seems to like it. He dribbles and claps. Jackson does the zip of the central pocket until Frank is snugly wrapped: a makeshift pram.

'Frank,' he says, 'are you listening? Mum is gone, I don't know where, and we have to find her. Understand?'

He tugs the plastic handle until the metal rods extend, then lifts the duffel and drags it a couple of feet. The wheels drag heavily against the carpet, but the duffel moves. Frank bounces and writhes in his bag, but the zip holds firm.

'Stay still,' says Jackson. 'We're going.'

Jackson's mother showed him the special way out, the route she takes to find the pool in the afternoon. While she swam, Jackson would sink into the shallow end and pretend he was a mutant, that the world had flooded, and he was the only one who could breathe underwater, suspended in the pool's blue depths, goggles biting the bridge of his nose. The route leads from the lift through two white doors and to an outdoor path flanked by wooden lattices, the white grids woven with sweet-smelling vines. Flowers with yellow needles dot the leaves. The air smells like syrup as he drags Frank towards the road.

The high sun frazzles the valley's plants to browned bundles of gnarled, contorted leaves. Cacti bristle in the dirt. Bushes shiver with paper-pale leaves. Jackson took his father's tortoiseshell sunglasses, but the heavy-framed things keep slipping loose off his head. His eye-muscles ache in the light. Sweat wicks down his nose and sun-cream seeps into his lips, an acrid taste that makes him gag. He pushes the glasses up with one hand and uses the other to drag the case. A sharp pain spreads along his left arm. It feels as though the bones will snap, the joints collapse, the muscles unravel.

Frank dozes in the suitcase, stunned by heat. Jackson watches the trail of bright rocks, crooked as a lightning bolt, that runs along the floor of the valley. This is the path they must follow. It leads to the sea.

The sky and the earth are at war and the earth is losing. Bone-dry branches crackle under Frank's duffel as it drags. The ditch beside the road is filled with empty plastic bottles, wads of tissue, whitened cans, and limp bags muddled in the gravel. Black flies buzz over hay-studded lumps of dung.

Whatever survives in this heat, in this dust, is evil. Beetles clamber over stones and through mazes of knotted grass. Their gloss-black armour reflects the sky's punishing blue. A spiny thing scuttles under a rock, too fast for Jackson to see it properly. The rocks themselves are rubble, the sharp, half-pulverized remains of a recent explosion: a bomb dropped from the sky, a great wave of destructive heat. There are no birds. No bees. Just hardened, spiky creatures crawling through dirt in which no flowers will grow.

The road curves gently as it descends, tracing the bulk of the mountain. There is a bay in the town at the bottom, a harbour with bobbing boats. Jackson has never been so thirsty in his life. Hot air scorches his lips. His cells have hardened to grains of sand.

There is a cluster of trees near the road. They have lots of branches and even some leaves. Thin shapes shimmer in the heat pulsing off the stones. He drags Frank through big white boulders until they reach the shade. Frank reaches out and grabs a handful of empty air. A sweet, rancid smell hangs around him.

Jackson lifts Frank down from his throne, lays him on the earth, and tugs the sellotapey bits on the side of his nappy. The nappy flops open to reveal a smeared dollop of yellow wet muck. Jackson tugs it off Frank and chucks it behind a bush. He grabs a fistful of fallen leaves, their waxy skins crisped at the edges, and wipes his brother clean.

'Okay,' says Jackson. 'Better.'

He gulps from the big plastic bottle he found on his mother's bedside table and filled from the tap before they left. The liquid slides down through him as he gulps, a clean, clear feeling that pools in his stomach and spreads through his blood. This is the best drink, the best in the world, he will never drink coke again. He puts the bottle to Frank's chapped lips and watches him swallow. Water spills down his grubby cheeks.

As soon as the water is finished, Frank begins to cry. The wail pierces Jackson's ears. 'Shut up,' he says, skull throbbing. 'Shut up. Shut up. *Shut up.*'

Naked from the waist down, Frank screams in the dirt.

Jackson is about to hit his brother, to kick him until his is quiet, until he remembers the powder. He unzips the netted pouch in the side of the duffel and takes out the second bottle. This one is filled with powdered, pre-mixed milk, the bottle's sides specked with its creamy white silt.

Frank takes the plastic nipple in his mouth and instantly falls quiet. A frown of intense concentration, or of blissful distraction, creases his features. He sucks with a rhythmic hunger, breathing through his nose, until the milk has gone. A moment later, he drops the bottle. His head lolls to one side.

A lizard darts up the side of a tree. It halts halfway and flicks its tongue, a trill of red against the brown wood. Jackson chews the bread roll he stole from the breakfast buffet and watches the lizard's stomach pulse as it breathes. Its small eye is fixed on his, a bright black bead. It slips into the crack of a broken stone and disappears.

Jackson lies beside his brother. His body aches all over, and although the sun is high, the light blinding, he can barely keep his eyes open. Warm air caresses his skin. He rests his head on his folded arm and listens to the crackling heat.

The sky fades from yellow to orange to purple, like a bonfire slowly dying. Now it is so blue it looks black, with a deep red scar in the distance. Too many stars to count: a sprinkling of cold bright points.

Now that dark is falling, Jackson is afraid of the road. The sudden, swooping flash of the headlamps. The thunder of exhaust. He has watched the cars roar down it, bright lights rippling past the rock. Adults. Strangers. Police. Anyone could see them, grab them, drag them back to the fortress hotel.

Instead of walking back to the tarmac, he turns the other way. It is darker in the valley, and the way is strewn with rocks. He drags the suitcase along the dried-up riverbed, between the boulders and the trees, heading towards the distant lights of the town. The duffel case jolts and bounces, it growls to a halt in the dirt or gets jammed between rocks. He has to stop repeatedly to set it free or pluck out the toothy stones that get stuck in its wheels.

Later, one of the wheels breaks off: a brief yelp of snapped plastic.

Jackson drags the broken bag for as long as he can but it's too heavy with just one wheel. He stands in a patch of sand, panting. The temperature is dropping in the valley. A breezeblock house stands nearby, its windows pitch dark.

'You need to get out,' he says, lifting Frank from the duffel.

Frank sits in the dirt and rubs his eyes.

'Thank you very much,' Jackson says. He is talking to the duffel, not his brother. It has taken them so far – down the road, across the valley.

He plucks a flower from the dirt. It has avocado-green leaves with sharp edges and a small white flower. He lays the flower in the suitcase, takes a handful of dirt and lets it slip from his hand to the edge of the weeping stem. He pours a dash of water on the dirt.

27

'Okay,' he tells Frank. 'We can go now.'

He drinks half the water and leaves the rest to his brother. Instead of crying, Frank watches Jackson with his wide, calm eyes.

The town is closer than Jackson realised, right there, beyond the trees. He can see its dark buildings and yellow lights. The hotel is far away, pale and solid in the night's blue heat.

Frank is usually good at crawling. But the rocks have the texture of sandpaper, his knees and wrists get scuffed. The moon is high above them now, a bright, pale face. Shadows stretch across the lightning bolt, the white stones smoothed by a vanished river. Jackson thinks about his mother. She will be happy when he finds her. She will smile, she will be proud.

But Frank is being stupid, too slow. He can't even walk: he just crawls along, lazy and aimless, with sudden whimpers and anguished howls. Jackson lifts Frank under the armpits and shows him how to do it.

'This foot,' he says, 'then the other foot, then the other foot again, like this.'

Frank concentrates very hard, but his legs jerk around like a puppet's. He puts his right foot down and wobbles. Jackson loosens his grip and Frank dumps down on the broad white stone and claps his hands.

Something moves through the sky. It looks to Jackson like a giant insect with a shiny, dark-orange shell. Its blades hum through the valley and fade and blend with the crickets' singing. A long white beam of light is shining from its head. The beam swings left and right, searching for something on the far side of the buildings, out at sea.

The rest of the walk has the feel of a dream, an endless stumble over warm stones and dusty stretches.

Then, without warning, they reach the edge of the town, a narrow path winding up to the street through twisted, bowing trees. The town is dark and mostly empty. Some people are in the restaurants at the bay, sitting outside on the porches, drinking and smoking cigarettes, laughter echoing off the walls and mixing with the hiss of the surf. Foreheads glistening. Big smiles.

Jackson looks for his mother for a very long time. He walks down empty streets and dark alleys, chasing stray shadows and sounds. Afraid of being seen, he hovers in doorways, but does not knock. Instead, he stands at windows. He glimpses a gloomy corridor through ghostly net curtains. Women slicing onions in a bright kitchen where a radio blares. A family gathered in front of the TV, slumped on sofas or wicker chairs. Two dogs running circles in an empty, white-tiled room. Delicious smells perfume the alleys: fried garlic, roasted meat. He walks along the harbour looking at restaurants, shops, and cafés until he reaches a narrow path leading into a copse of dark trees. But she wouldn't be there, in the forest. The shadows chitter. He turns to go.

Fishing boats sway in the water, chains rattling as waves knock their sides. The sea is black and silver in the light of the moon. The flying thing has disappeared but is buzzing somewhere, near the cliffs.

He stands outside the restaurants and peers through the open doors and goes inside the one with the candles. It is his mother's favourite place to eat. They have the freshest fish, she says – the owner's father is a fisherman. Jackson stands at the window, peering in. The room is empty. Chairs upside-down on the tables. A vague smell of smoke haunts the air. For a long time, he stands in the middle of the empty, lamp-lit room, surrounded by upturned furniture, and does nothing. He wants to give up. To stop looking. But how else is he meant to find her?

Earlier, Jackson had found a good place in an empty garden with crumbling walls and laid his brother down beside a bush in a wooden trough filled with dead leaves. Frank is sleeping when Jackson returns. The garden is quiet. Creatures scuttle and slip through the grass, insects dance in the air. Jackson sits beside his brother and cries.

When he is finished he carries Frank over the crumbled wall and into the dim amber street and sits him down. Frank is half asleep, making vague and sleepy movements with his arms. His drooping head rests against the stone wall.

'It's your fault,' Jackson says. 'You weren't strong enough. You weren't old enough. You were *stupid*.'

He slaps Frank on the head. Frank's face scrunches up and he starts to cry, a throaty wail that fills the alley.

'If you weren't here, I would have found her,' Jackson says. 'Stupid, stupid, *stupid* Frank. *Your* fault.'

There is movement at the edge of his vision. He turns to see his mother at the end of the street, levitating mid-air. His heart stutters and a bright light bursts in his head. Then his eyes adjust to the glare of the lamps. It is a woman, another stranger, not his mother after all. She has long dark hair and is sitting in a chair made from red plastic. It is raised off the street on black wheels.

'Hey,' the woman says, 'are you alright?'

She is English but has a strong accent. She isn't from Jackson's city. Her necklace sparkles in the electric light.

Frank is wailing now. Water streams down his red cheeks. The brothers look at the woman.

'I'm really tired,' Jackson says.

'Oh,' she replies. 'I'm sorry to hear that.'

She wears a dark red dress and high heels. A handbag hangs from the handle at the back of her chair.

'Who's that?' she asks.

'Frank,' Jackson says.

'I like his T-shirt,' the woman replies. 'Are you lost?'

Jackson nods. He doesn't have the energy to run.

'That's sad,' the woman says. Crickets whirr across the valley. Jackson listens to the hush of the waves. 'I heard something on the radio earlier,' she says. 'It said the police were looking for two young boys. I don't suppose you know where they are?'

'No,' Jackson says.

'Apparently they went missing from the hotel this afternoon.'

Jackson blinks. 'Okay.'

'Well,' she says, 'you must be tired.'

'I am.'

'Being tired is boring.'

Frank stops crying, a bewildered look on his tear-soaked face.

'What is that?' Jackson asks, nodding at the wheels of her chair.

'Oh,' the woman says, 'it's my chair. Look.' She moves the small stick on the arm. The chair jerks left, then right. It makes a whirring sound.

'Why do you have it?'

'To get around.'

'What's wrong with your legs?'

The woman laughs. 'I was sick when I was little,' she says. 'About the same size as your brother.'

'He can't walk either.'

The woman laughs again. Her voice is clear and bright, like a note high up on a piano. 'He will one day.

Look, he's already moving around.'

'He goes in the wrong direction. He keeps stopping to pick things up. He falls asleep.'

The woman shrugs. 'Could be worse.'

Frank is lifting his foot to his open mouth and attempting to eat the big toe. The foot is covered in dirt. Jackson bats it away and tells his brother to stop.

'I think we need to get you back home,' the woman says. 'I would want to be back home, if I was down a strange dark road.'

The town is fast asleep. Home is very far away.

'Why are you here?' Jackson says.

'Oh, well... I was at a nightclub.'

'What's a nightclub?'

'A place where people go to be awful human beings,' the woman says. She stares at the moon for a while, as if deep in thought. 'I've realized that I don't like my friends. I think the feeling is mutual. It's a bit sad, really, isn't it? An awkward thing to discover when you're sharing a house with them for another ten days.' The lady digs in her bag while she talks. She pulls out a mobile phone and prods a button. 'How about we call someone? I think that would be – FUCK!' The woman yells. 'Wait – sorry – language. Reception around here – it's total shit.'

Jackson feels suddenly, painfully hungry, as though he hasn't eaten in weeks.

'Listen,' the woman says. 'I'm staying just up the road. It's not far. I could carry your brother on the chair, and maybe you too, if you hang on the back.'

'That?' says Jackson, pointing.

'It's faster than it looks. You'd be surprised.'

The coastal road edges the foothills, overlooking the town and the sea. The wind is warm. It smells of dead leaves and ground pepper. Anita was right – her chair is faster than it looks. All she has to do is push the lever forward and it zooms like a rocket. Jackson stands on a thin metal shelf on the back. He grips the plastic handles either side of the chair, which are sculpted for larger fingers than his. The breeze rushes through his hair and he feels like he's flying, a bird in the night. He lets out a long, high scream. The wind roars in his open mouth and teases tears from his eyes. Anita laughs and he forgets where he is: there is only their laughter, the smell of shampoo, and strange hair in his teeth. Now and then a car rushes past and the road glows white. Then the car will disappear and darkness will swallow the road.

Frank is asleep in Anita's lap, wrapped in her coat. Her hair flutters in Jackson's face as the wind shifts. Now and then she shouts things at him. She asks him what food he likes.

'Rice,' he says. 'Yellow melon. Calamari.'

'What would you like to be when you grow up?'

'A man from space.'

'An astronaut?'

He shakes his head. 'A man from space.'

'You're an interesting boy,' Anita says.

Jackson's eyes are fixed on the side of the road. His mother might be waiting in the shadows under the trees, or beside the rocks: in the secret chambers of the land, like where the lizard vanished earlier. But the steeper the road, the more his gaze is tugged towards the moonlit blackness of the sea, which is bigger than everything, which swallows the sky.

A jolt makes Anita's chair jump. She shrieks wildly; Jackson laughs.

'That's where I'm staying,' she shouts. A short way down the road is a row of buildings, their front gardens crowded with spiky palms. 'We'll be there in a jiffy.' She says the last bit in a funny accent, with a silly posh twang.

A convertible car drives down the road in the same direction. Five men and two women are crammed into it, shouting and laughing. Two women are perched on the back where the roof is folded, bottles in their hands. The men wear the collars of their polo shirts up; the women wear dresses with straps. The car slows to a crawl beside Anita's chair.

'Fuckin' hell!' says one of the men.

'What the fuck *is* that?' says another.

They are from Jackson's city.

'Leave it off,' says one of the women.

'Looks like a tank fucked a baby chair.'

A few start laughing. The exhaust tastes bitter, burnt.

'Haven't you got better things to do?' Anita yells.

'Saw her on the edge of the dance floor,' one of them shouts, 'and I was like – who invited Stephen Hawking?'

The country beyond the road is very dark. Anita's building looked close before. Now it is far away.

'She's got a baby with her.'

'Fuck me, it spawned!'

'I said leave it off!'

'She nicked them. She zooms around snatching kids in her chair – like some fuckin' – like some fuckin'...'

'Come on,' Anita shouts, 'say something funny.'

Another car pulls up behind the convertible. It honks its horn several times and the driver yells in Spanish.

The convertible accelerates. The women on the back aren't wearing seatbelts. They shriek as the car speeds off, almost tumbling onto the road. One of them lets go of her cigarette, which sheds a trail of dying sparks as it flies. Soon both cars are gone and the road is empty again, the bare rocks silent at the side of the tarmac.

Anita's house is very large. In the tiled living room there is a big TV, white leather furniture, an indoor bar, and an aquarium. Bright fish swim around branching coral, wavering water plants, and purple rocks. Outside, through the glass windows, deck chairs are placed round a swimming pool. On low wooden tables around the pool are bottles and narrow glasses, bowls of olives and plates of crusty bread.

Jackson carries Frank to the sofa and sits beside him. The leather creaks. Anita makes a phone call in the corridor. Her voice sounds muffled down the hall. She rolls into the living room, parks her chair beside the other sofa, and hauls herself onto it using her arms. Her leg gets caught on the sofa's arm; she lifts it over then smoothes her dress out over her thighs.

'Do you need me to help?' Jackson asks.

'It's fine,' she says. 'This is nothing. But thanks.'

She pours herself white wine and asks Jackson if he is thirsty. 'Help yourself,' she says, pointing at the open door.

In the kitchen he drinks a huge glass of water then fills the glass up again and carries it into the living room. He pours a little into Frank's mouth, even though he's half asleep. Frank swallows and stretches his arms.

'Someone's coming to collect you,' Anita says. 'They sounded relieved.'

Jackson nods. 'Who were those people? The ones on the road.'

'Oh,' says Anita. '*Them.*' She takes a big mouthful from her glass, a distant look on her face. 'People with cruel hearts and low IQs. Lottie included.'

'Who is that?'

'The one on the back. She met a tribe of cognitively challenged primates at the place we were at before.'

'The woman in the car was your friend?'

Anita finds this funny. 'Exactly,' she says. 'Past tense.'

Dog-eared magazines are raggedly stacked on the coffee table. There are bottles and glasses everywhere, beer and wine, and napkins with olive pips and smears of lipstick on them. Earlier, Anita had opened the big French windows. The room is filled with the lull of the sea. Jackson stares across the pool at the darkness beyond. Specks of light are swirling, stars or insects: hard to tell.

The doorbell cries out. Jackson runs to answer it, convinced that it will be her: mousy hair at her shoulders, smile wide under pale brown eyes, purse and car keys clutched in her hands, and the particular smell of her skin at her neck when she hugs him – biscuity, sandy-sweet, warm. He yanks open the door, heart pounding, a grin twisting his face. Something plummets in his chest. It's a couple, but they aren't his parents. Blue uniforms. Black caps.

'You!' the woman snaps. 'Why did you go off like that?'

'Are you insane?' says the man. 'Where is your brother?'

'It was very bad thing you did,' says the woman, 'very bad, very childish. You just like him, is that it? Your father? We all completely lose our—'

'I want my dad,' Jackson says.

The policeman's expression changes. 'Well, maybe you don't want to see him. Not now what he did. Very stupid, very bad. We try and understand where this comes from, but...' He shrugs.

'Still,' says the woman, smiling at Jackson, 'we're glad you're okay.'

She does not sound glad.

'What did he do?' Jackson asks. 'Where is he?'

The policeman ignores his question. 'There was a woman who rang, earlier?' asks the man. He has taken his hat off. His black fringe is flattened, glossy with sweat. 'Is she inside?'

When the policeman sees Anita's chair, he halts and says: 'Oh.'

Bent at the waist, he holds his hand out for her to shake, which she does.

'Thank you so much. I mean—' he chuckles '—really.' He goes to pick up Frank but Jackson leaps between them.

'Don't touch him,' Jackson snaps. He will carry his brother himself.

Jackson mumbles thanks to Anita, who tells him: 'Any time.' She smiles but looks tired. There is a brief silence before the policeman steps forward.

'Alright,' he says. 'Now we get in the car.'

The road twists away from the town along the steep rocky parts of the land, and the world grows smaller as they rise. Soon the valley looks like a map: blurry humps and lakes of shadow, dotted lights that look like fires. There are mountains in the distance, saw-tooth gaps where there aren't any stars. At the bottom of the valley is the riverbed, white stones aglow in the light of the moon. The journey felt so hot and so long that they would die before it ended, but now it looks as thin and insignificant as a snail's trail. He rests his head against the window. The car's engine purrs in his skull. Frank is fast asleep. Jackson leans over and touches his brother's hot head. He tries to send him a message, but the police will not shut up. They chatter noisily in Spanish. The woman throws her head back and laughs, her bared teeth reflected in the windshield. There is a bend in the road and the headlamps make a pale tree glow. Soon the hotel is visible, a silhouette against the moonlit sky. Jackson cradles Frank's head in his arms. He ducks into the shadows and shuts his eyes.

II. LESSONS

Tuesday morning. Double English. Old poems. Jackson lurks in the back of Learning Suite 7 with his head hanging low. He doodles a boat in the margins and quivers with scorn for his classmates, existence, the world. Hayley – hockey star, budding smoker, setter of trends – is sitting beside him.

'Oi,' she stage-whispers, 'my pen broke. Pass me yours.'

A blank expression is Jackson's answer: he stares at her wide brown eyes.

Hayley erupts. 'What the fuck is wrong with you?' she yells, face screwed in a scowl of repulsion.

The instructor snaps a warning, but Hayley has a point. What *is* wrong with Jackson?

When he was younger, he often flew into inexplicable rages, but these have steadily begun to subside: his violent outbursts have been subsumed into an eerie air of vigilant reservation, of monkish quiet. Some of the instructors have diagnosed him as mute; others 'on the spectrum'. Others still have been stunned by his work. They praise him in the margins – 'Excellent!!', 'Powerfully argued!' – but express concern about his pessimism, jabbing him with questions after class. He answers easily, if quietly, somewhat stiltedly, picking his way from word to word. She makes encouraging noises. She calls him a 'dark horse'. He must try to speak more in class.

Jackson stares at the photocopied poem, which, the instructor explained at the start of the lesson, was written in the seventeenth century. The poet believed in God, which means the poet must have been stupid. Two lines sharpen into focus, distilling themselves from the fog of Jackson's impulsive but total dismissal of the poem.

My mirth and edge was lost, a blunted knife
Was of more use than I.

Despite his abiding suspicion that poetry is a grandiose conspiracy of words, whose function is to enshrine the authority of the instructors who teach them, the lines trigger something in Jackson. He reads them again, again. They resound in his head like a mantra, and he is troubled by the changes they bring. He scribbles circles around the word 'knife' until it resembles a malevolent sun that sheds concentric ripples, scratched ink that blackens the page.

A siren announces the lesson's end. He waits for the room to clear before slipping outside.

Dust-haze hangs across the field as students skirmish, fighting or playing football, it's hard to tell. Jackson heads round the back of the Annexe, where two younger students, crouched in the murk of the huge dead bush, are fumbling a lighter and a joint. He slips round the thorny ruins of the droughted rosebeds that edge the outer wall, and climbs into the tree where he's arranged to meet Frank. A shell of leaves surrounds him, chopping the sun to soft coins of light. Carved names scar the trunk. Scorched roaches are wedged in the cracks of the branches.

Frank will be five minutes, at least; longer if he's done something bad. Jackson rests his head against the trunk and shuts his eyes.

Some people find it hard to believe that the brothers are brothers. While Jackson prickles at the edges, blank-faced or scowling, and more or less mute, Frank is a show-off, an extrovert. He joined the District Institute this year and has been wreaking gleeful havoc ever since. He dances on desks and sets fire alarms wailing;

he graffitis elaborate though anatomically improbable dicks, fannies, and faces on corridor walls. He runs rings around his instructors – actual rings, tiny dizzying circuits, like a crazed dog chasing its tail.

Leonard diagnosed boredom.

'It's simple, isn't?' Leonard snapped. 'He's smart. He need something to do – not a bunch of jobsworth cretins ramming propaganda down his throat.'

The N.D.I. wouldn't, or couldn't, give Frank 'something to do'. His behaviour got worse. Once, during French, he jumped on a table, stripped naked, and howled like a wolf: '*Yeee ooooo ooooo oooo oo wo wow oooooooo wwwwwwwwwwwwww!*' The red-faced instructor tried and failed to tame Frank, but he was naked, it was awkward, and pretty soon the tears were rolling down her face. His classmates cackled, gawped, and no-fucking-wayed. He scribbled tattoos on his face and chest with a marker, and jumped from chair to chair.

'*Aaaaaaa oo woooooo oooooo hhhhhhh www ooo owwwww-wwwww woooooo oooooo oooo ooooo ohhhhh hhhh rrr ghhhh h!*'

Jackson is quietly impressed by his brother's behaviour: the elaborate lies and fantastical stories, his cheerful indifference to punishment.

And then there is the man Frank repeatedly draws, in notebooks and on corridor walls: a looming figure with a blank, faceless head and a blue-and-white striped shirt. Frank insists the man, called Arkady, is real; that he visits him in his dreams: a strange protector or vengeful foe. Frank began drawing him a while back, around the time the brothers moved into Leonard's flat.

Jackson remembers, or thinks he remembers, the night they arrived, unannounced, at the door. Frank, in his yellow poncho, was holding Jackson's hand. He remembers the pattern of rainwater pooled on the

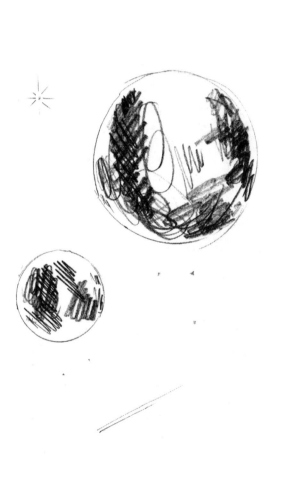

floor: the image is like a photograph, clear and precise. Leonard loomed in the opened doorway, stick-thin and crookedly stooped, his bright eyes hooded in cavernous sockets. He glowered at the boys:

'No fucking way.'

Frank's favourite lesson, the only one he really behaves in, is Art. He loves the wide, scuffed desks that stretch beneath shelves of charcoal, chalk, newsprint, and paint; he loves the riverbed stink of wet clay as he mushes and tugs it into crocodiles, lions' heads, submarines. The instructor lets him work on his private projects: posters for made-up films, illustrations of Arkady.

'Hey.'

Frank is in the branches' shadow, squinting up at Jackson and clutching a long stick like a staff. He looks, from this height, even skinnier than usual. The T-shirt draped on his shoulders hangs loose round his whippet-thin torso, and his trousers are rolled at the ankles, swaying as he leans on his stick.

'You're late,' says Jackson.

'Yeeeeeeeeeaaaah,' says Frank, kicking a pebble across the dry grass. His dark hair, shiny with sweat, crawls over his forehead and into his eyes. 'There was a thing.'

'A thing?'

'A lizard.'

Jackson sighs. 'There wasn't a lizard.'

'There was! It went like that,' Frank makes a scuttling motion with his hand, 'all the way up the side of the Exercise Hall.'

Jackson slips off the branch and lands with a smack on the root-riddled earth. 'Why are you being a dickhead?' he snaps. 'If you're going to be a prick about this, the lesson is cancelled, you're staying here.'

'I wasn't even that late.'

Arms folded, Jackson scowls at his brother. He is aware of the Institute's bulk, its huge structures and unreadable windows, its screaming pupils and conspiring cliques, its warrens of portakabins and raggedy stretches of unkempt grass, but his attention is focused elsewhere: the abandoned office with its vast grey floors and its light-flooded windows.

'Plllleeeeeeeaaaaaaaase,' Frank whines. His stick clatters to the ground as he clasps his hands. 'I'm not a dickhead. I'm not! Tell me what to do.'

Jackson scans the street from the top deck. His eye lingers on buildings he's recently opened: the flat above the corner shop, the garage round the back of the creepy hotel with the permanent VACANCIES. His explorations have expanded; he ventures further and further afield. He pushes east through the city's post-industrial districts, the warehouses converted into craft beer saloons or flattened altogether, until he hits the misty marshes on the city's outer zones; west through a maze of neon, through the avenues of china-white townhouses, and into the tree-cushioned suburbs beyond; south through shopping villages, golf courses and ragged graveyards; or north past MOT garages piled with tyres, thatched-roof pubs and chain hotels until the orbital motorway roars. He sees things. Mountains of wooden pallets ablaze at night in a derelict yard. A man in a Snow White costume passed out in the dead centre of a four-lane road. A street lined with cars in which people are sleeping, empty tins of baked beans on the dashboards, clothes stuffed into bin bags or heaped in open cases, the glass opaque with condensing breath.

He rests his head against the window, soothed by the hum of the glass. Frank scratches a face into the back of the seat in front using pencil.

Part of Jackson wishes he was back at Leonard's, curled up and warm on the floor. Before the Institute, before the Dragon entered their life, Leonard taught Jackson simple things. How to chop vegetables, how to fry meat. He took Jackson to the supermarket, gave him a fiver, and told him to buy stuff for dinner: he blew the first budget on iced buns, chocolates, and magazines. Outside, in public spaces, while Frank played on the swings, Leonard taught Jackson boxing. He lifted his pale, bony palms and told Jackson to punch them, left-right-left. Once, when they were younger, they travelled by train to a campsite. There was a lake nearby. Leonard took them swimming in water so cold it robbed the breath from their lungs when they leaped into the weedy shallows. He asked them if they trusted him, told them to hold their breaths, and held their heads underwater. They didn't drown. They rowed across the water in a tiny wooden boat. The sky was cloudless, blazing bright. They lay in the boat while it drifted, trailing their hands in the cool, dark water. As they walked the wood's paths padded with pine needles, he taught them how to make shelter. He stripped a pair of branches with a penknife and rested them against a tree. Across the triangular structure, he laid longer branches with leaves on them, forming a slanted roof. Jackson and Frank helped out. Soon there was a kind of tent. They climbed inside and sat in the darkness that smelled of cut leaves and dank soil. Leonard's furry hat looked silly on his skull-like face. They roasted marshmallows on the ends of sticks and ate the sticky, goo-filled lumps of pink and white, and Jackson felt happy, and Frank was laughing, and Leonard was almost asleep against a tree, with the sound of a stream in the distance, under the shelter they had made.

Then came the Dragon, the wheezing: red phlegm and blue pills.

The brothers jump off the bus. The office is a short walk under the flyover, the shadows swirling with exhaust as cars roar by.

'Can we do more climbing?' Frank asks. He grips the gnawed corners of his jumper in his teeth, tugging more fibres loose. 'We going somewhere new?'

Jackson shakes his head. 'We're practising maps.'

'*Maps*? I know all about maps.' He kicks a crushed can and watches it skitter.

'These are different,' says Jackson. 'You'll draw them.'

'Oh,' says Frank, sounding sceptical, before his face brightens into a wicked smile. 'Okay. I'm good at that.'

Timing is crucial. You have to be sly. You can't just smash a window or jump a fence in broad daylight, condemned in the glare of the public's presumption. Jackson leads his brother down the road, but the pavements are busy. He ducks into a doorway and pretends to check his phone.

Jackson gets physically sick of it sometimes: chesty cough, inexplicable nausea, aching bones. Broken windows bite his palms as he boosts the sills. He sprains his ankles on crooked stairs. There are pointless fights when he steps on someone's turf, pointless fights if they step on his. Sometimes his nostrils recoil at a familiar, high-pitched, rotten-sour smell, which he hopes is rancid milk but is almost certainly something worse. The rooms are scattered with sadness and waste: fading photographs, blackened pipes.

But pain is an education. Beneath, beside, between

the city's official boundaries – its maps of space, which are maps of ownership, maps of property, maps of power – other territories and signals appear: an infinity of codes that dictate how the city is moved through, immaterial borders that constantly rise and fall and flux, like tides. Sometimes he'll be struck by a delirious dread that makes his fingers and forearms fizz. His heartbeat spikes and his throat feels strangled by invisible hands. He doesn't think he might *possibly* be about to die – he *knows* he is: of a heart attack or aneurysm or some medically unprecedented eruption of guts and blood that will need washing clean with industrial hoses. Lights quiver and swim. His skin prickles with inexplicable pain.

When it passes – it always eventually passes, leaving the promise of death unfulfilled – Jackson tells no one, not even Frank.

The lessons take place in the evenings, at weekends, and in the adrenalized afternoons when the brothers bunk off. Jackson teaches Frank about his secret life, his rides to the city's four corners, and passes down secret knowledge. The point of the lessons, Jackson says, is survival. Unlike 'trigonometry' or 'extended metaphor', the word makes immediate sense. Frank feels the word in his fingers, rolls it under his tongue. He slips survival into his pocket: a secret, a weapon, a hex.

The alley – grubby and dark, nothing special – juts off a long main road lined with anonymous blocks and chain cafés. Bin bags, heaped in squishy mounds, leak tarry juice; the runoff dribbles through a grille and into the tubes and tunnels of the city's swollen bowels.

Frank pictures the Maths class he's supposed to be in right now, students half asleep over pages of gridded paper. He beams.

They scrabble over hoarding adorned with photos of couples smiling in fake rooms, and duck into the dusty hush beside the tall building. Pellets of fox droppings litter the ground, the only sign that anything else is alive. Frank glances at the entrance to one of the buildings, where he spray-painted their secret logo: two heads, in profile, beneath a radiant crown.

The seventh floor of the office building is a clone of all the others, vacant, pale, and flooded with light from the strip of windows. The space is empty, derelict. Dark patches where desks, cupboards, printers, photocopiers, potted plants and water coolers once stood now pattern the sun-bleached carpet. Half-dismantled desks and chairs litter the floor. Wires hang tangled from vanished ceiling tiles. Frank sits on his office chair, shoes dangling an inch above the carpet. He folds his hands on the desk's speckled plastic veneer and looks up at his brother. Jackson pulls the stuff from his rucksack, lays it neatly on the desk.

'You ready?' he asks.

'Yep,' says Frank. He taps the pencil on the desk and bites his lip, taps it, taps again.

'Stop it,' his brother says. 'Drives me insane when you do that.'

The squint with which Jackson pierces the window's glare makes his forehead crease like an older man's. For a while he stands there watching, momentarily transfixed by something outside.

'Okay,' he says, 'remember where we got to last week?'

Frank nods.

'Good,' says Jackson. 'I want you to try again. Where we finished last time. Same instructions. Just start again, like nothing's happened in between.'

'Okay. Got it. Fine.'

Frank arranges four sheets of paper across the desk so they form a larger page. The graphite hovers over the bottom right corner. He draws a line across the middle, another one up the side. He doesn't know what he's doing. The pencil meanders around the page.

Frank has arranged a handful of treasured objects on the desk: the glass turtle, the blue bottle, the mirror-shard, and the round, grey pebble. He stares at the latter for inspiration, willing it to give him ideas. Its pale grey surface, smoothed by water to a perfect ovoid resembling a gull's egg, is speckled white. He found the stone on the street a few weeks ago, when the sun was setting fire to the dazzling windows, which flashed the light back red and gold. Something about the stone had struck Frank, in that moment, as significant. Its rounded smoothness. Its balanced weight. Mostly he loves the speckled pattern, the white dots flecked throughout the dark grey. He believed, at the time, that the stone was a map of the night sky, a constellation inscribed on a pebble, but now that he is here he sees the stone for what it is: a meaningless lump.

These aren't the only lessons Jackson gives, but they're definitely the weirdest. Most of the lessons are practical, hands-on. How to crowbar open a fire escape, short-circuit certain alarms, or scavenge food. Combined with these are lessons of a more abstract, even philosophical nature. They are, Jackson grandly proclaims, an 'antidote to official knowledge'. For months, he taught Frank a course called 'How to Read the News', the central tenet being 'don't trust a word'. The lessons left Frank's brain feeling scrambled, numb with boredom.

'Finished,' says Frank, squinting at the page.

Jackson wanders over and inspects the pencilled lines. They branch and veer in random directions, a tentacular node of squiggles and scrawls. Frank chews the end of a pencil and watches his brother. It's not a good start. He could do better, has done better in the past.

'This is bollocks,' Jackson says, chucking the pages onto the floor. 'What is this meant to say?'

Frank frowns, shame pulsing through his body like heat.

'It doesn't say anything,' he says. 'It's a *picture.*'

'Do it again.'

Four clean sheets, arranged in a square. The pencil hovers over the page.

This time he thinks about a trip they took last summer, to the beach. The brothers cycled down the long, bleak coastal roads under mountainous, black-bottomed clouds. Reeds rustled at the tarmac's fringe. Coast wind pounded the bikes so hard he'd had to lean all the way to one side. On the beach at night, they made a fire. Slivers of driftwood spat sparks.

'Here,' he says, pushing back from the desk.

Jackson inspects Frank's second attempt. The drawing is somehow tighter, its edges more distinct. They contain something. It's hard to know what, exactly, but it's there.

'This is better,' says Jackson. 'Much better. I can imagine this place is real.'

'It *is* real,' says Frank.

Jackson ignores his brother in favour of his phone. 'Alright. One good, one shit. Let's have a break.'

Frank lies flat on his back. He whistles an aimless, meandering tune, inhaling the stewed-air smell of the room. He slaps the carpet tile. A cloud of particles leap and wander weightlessly, catching the light.

'Alright,' Jackson says a moment later. 'Get up.'

'The ceiling looks so weird from here,' says Frank,

looking at the pockmarked white of the tiles. 'Like the surface of the moon.'

'Get up. We haven't finished.'

'I'm hungry,' says Frank.

'Already?' Silence. 'You can eat when we're done.'

Frank sits back on the chair and glowers at Jackson.

'I want you to do something different this time,' Jackson says. 'This one isn't like the other lessons. I want you to draw a map of a place that doesn't exist.'

'What do you mean?' says Frank.

'Just imagine a place,' says Jackson, 'and draw it.'

Frank is confused at first. He doesn't know if Jackson is playing a joke, but his brother's face, as usual, gives nothing away. Jackson stands at Frank's shoulder and stares at the blank page, so close that he can hear the flutey sounds his brother's nose makes when he breathes.

'What are you waiting for?' says Jackson.

The room is vast and stark, interrupted here and there by thick white columns supporting the ceiling. Dead spider plants are racked along the windowsill; they cast long, spindly shadows on the floor like witches' spell-casting hands. Frank is overcome by the sense that someone else used to sit right here, at this empty desk in this corpse of a building, a person with a suit, a family, a name, a salary, a job, probably a mortgage, certainly a body – a body that pressed its weight into this faux-leather cushion, slathered it in sweat, grease, shed cells and dead hair.

'I don't know what to draw,' he says.

'Just make it up,' says Jackson. 'It's the easiest thing in the world.'

Frank leans over the desk, his eyes fixed on the space between the pencil and the page, a gap that seems impossible to cross when Jackson is standing right there beside him, observing his every move. Frank waits for an idea but nothing arrives. He thinks about cities, fields, forests and motorways, all the kinds of places he drew so easily as a kid. The shapes shift and dissolve at such high speed that all he can see inside his head is a flickering, fading blur.

'I can't do it,' he says.

Jackson is a silhouette. Arms folded, he tilts his head.

'The sooner you do it, the sooner it's over.'

Frank rubs his itching eyes with the knuckles of both hands.

A drawing is just a drawing, a mess of scribbles on a page: if Jackson wanted a pretty picture then he could search for one online. Frank lowers the tip of his pencil.

'Remember what we said before,' says Jackson, 'about starting with somewhere you know, then moving outwards.'

'I did that,' says Frank, 'just now. I used all the memory up.'

'Try again,' Jackson says.

Frank shuts his eyes and makes an effort to remember. Soon the images come flickering past.

He sees himself in an alley with Jackson, crouching, grit digging into their shoeless feet, gnawing a heel of bread. The bread is stale and has a rim of filth along its crust.

The public library, Jackson beside him, reading him books.

In Leonard's bathroom after the boiler broke, their clothes in a bucket, forearms beetroot-red in the icy water. The water clouds with the dirt leeching out of their clothes.

At the gates of the North District Institute, first day, feeling sick, surrounded by cackling crowds.

That time Jackson dislocated a kid's jaw after he pushed Frank; the way the kid's tongue flapped loose in his screaming mouth.

Running headlong from blackvests and laughing breathlessly when they escape.

The tongue-numbing taste of too much salt on kebab-shop chips.

Soon he is drawing quickly, fluently, sunk in his work. The feeling is specific but hard to define: he is anxious, excited, calm, all the moods mixed up together, swirling in his stomach and head. Instead of a place, he draws a home. It isn't an island. It doesn't have volcanoes, helipads or sprawling malls; there aren't any lakes or caves. He draws a square, and, within it, a smaller square. The space is sealed. He divides the interior with three horizontal lines, adding stairs between the floors, then beds, a bath, and windows, and pictures on the walls. Something isn't right. He erases the roof and adds more floors.

'This is good,' says Jackson – but Frank isn't really listening.

His pencil makes a shuffling sound. The tip becomes blunt as he works, soft lead fuzzing the lines. It feels like time is passing but it's hard to be sure. Frank glances around the room; the long, low, panelled bench-like thing beneath the window, the wall's hard corners and the packets of cement, or is it sand, stacked against a pillar.

Jackson places a plastic cup of water beside Frank's pages.

'I hate it when you do that,' says Frank.

'What?'

'Come over before I've finished.'

Jackson wanders back to the door. He leans against

the jamb, head cocked, smiling.

'Let me finish the balcony,' Frank says. He sketches the last few railings, more rapidly than he'd like, and pulls back from the desk. The drawing isn't finished. But Jackson is at his shoulder now, lifting the page to the light.

'This is good,' says Jackson. 'This is the best one yet.'

Frank stands up in his chair and spreads his arms wide: 'I'm the fucking champion! Oof oof oof,' he says, shadow-boxing the air. Jackson's face is slack, unimpressed, almost *disappointed*. 'Sorry,' Frank mutters, jogging circles on the floor. Pins and needles in his thighs: he has been sitting down too long.

'Did you do what I said,' says Jackson, 'and think about somewhere real?'

'Uh-huh,' Frank says. He picks a stray page off the floor: *FTG recently exported some thirty per cent of its workforce to China to leverage.* He crushes the paper into a ball.

'Which place did you think about?' says Jackson, still inspecting the page.

'The house.'

'Which house?'

Frank kicks the paper ball against a column. It bounces off and comes to rest in a tangle of wires. 'You *know* which one,' he says.

Frank liked to drag the sofa away from the wall in Leonard's flat to form a private, protected cave. He taped sheets of paper to the wall and spent hours drawing over them, pencil-and-crayon vistas. As he grew older, he started working in collage, cutting out photos from magazines and gluing them to the pages. Jackson would tell him what to draw, show him pages from comic books for inspiration: *draw a city*, he'd say; *draw a skyscraper, draw a fight breaking out on the street.* Often he drew Arkady:

the tall, faceless man who could fly through the air and travel through time. When Frank got bored, or the mural was finished, he would rip the drawings down and start again. He must have built and razed several cities, created and destroyed entire continents over the years.

One afternoon the brothers sat together in the warm dark of the fabric cave with a packet of biscuits between them. Frank pointed at a drawing on the wall. It showed a lone house floating high above a city, held aloft by engines shooting flared petals of blue and yellow crayon.

'I want to live here,' said Frank. 'That's my best house.'

Frank took Jackson on a tour of his imagined building: huge garden, penthouse cinema, games room, water slide.

'It's pretty great,' said Jackson. Then he noticed a problem. 'How would you get places?' The door opened onto thin air: if you stepped out, you'd drop to your death. 'And where would your shit go?' Frank looked nonplussed. 'The pipes in the bathroom need to go somewhere, don't they?' Jackson said. 'Or do they just leak out the bottom of the house and fall on everyone?' The idea made him smile. 'And what about water, for taps and showers? I don't see any pipes.'

'You get water from the clouds. The poo just goes...' Frank thought about it for a moment. '*Bang*!' he said.

'I don't think it works like that,' said Jackson.

'It does in my house,' said Frank.

Jackson packs the folded drawings away in his rucksack. The brothers jog down the windowless stairwell, footfall echoing off the bare walls, and slide into the reddening evening. Leonard's flat is near the top of a tower that from a distance resembles a breezeblock, a thump of solid grey. Its wide windows overlook a scrubby, nubbled park and the smog-softened reach of the city beyond it. The yard below is hushed as the brothers approach, the balconies crowded with wardrobes, shipping barrels, pigeon-roosts, clothes lines, rusting bikes. Jackson squints at Leonard's, a dim cave. His balcony is a miniature jungle, thronged with lush growths spilling out of their pots, several of which hang on chains from the ceiling, ivy trailing down like hair.

In the lobby, he presses the button to call the lift. The LED screen flashes dumbly: E-E-E.

'Not ag*ain*,' Frank groans, rolling his eyes.

The brothers climb the narrow stairwell, thighs aching, grumpy with hunger, until they reach the twenty-first floor. A striplight twitches in the corridor. Canned laughter, muffled by a neighbour's front door, reaches the brothers' ears.

Leonard is at the stove, whistling atonally to an advert. The TV is perched on the barstool in the corner, wires trailing out to a daisy-chained extension cable. His walking stick is propped against the fridge, his rain mac draped across the door of an open cupboard. Packets of food are piled up in the corner: bags of potatoes, out-of-date ready meals, bricks of cheese.

'Where you been?' he asks, without turning to greet them. His hair is so thin it almost doesn't exist: it hangs like a layer of fog around the wrinkly dome of his skull.

'Football,' Jackson sighs. 'Bumped into some mates in the park.'

'Bollocks,' Leonard replies.

His skin is dappled with liver spots, freckles, and moles. On hot days, slumped in his deck chair, he snoozes in the wedge of heat that falls through the balcony door. He doesn't walk so much as prowl, head low, knees bent, eyes searching. His incisors are uncommonly sharp.

Frank once called him Leopard. The nickname stuck. The flat was the Leopard's lair.

The lair is small enough that words like 'living room' and 'bedroom' have lost their meaning. Sometimes the brothers eat dinner on Leonard's creaking bed, other times in the living room, surrounded by towers of cardboard boxes filled with the broken electrical goods Leonard fixes and resells to supplement his pension. Sometimes they sit in the kitchen and watch TV, which shows the brothers an unfamiliar world: aster footage of burning tower blocks, glitchy phone recordings of random attacks, politicians at podiums. Tonight, the TV is on, so they will eat in the tiny kitchen. Steam condenses on the ceiling in yellowish drips.

'Give me a hand,' says Leonard, and Jackson slouches over.

Dinner is fried tomatoes draped in ribbons of blackened onion, served with boiled rice and white beans. Jackson drools like a dog at the prospect of food. Leonard wheezes, his leathery neck expanding and contracting with each inhale, fingers flexing as he works.

'Your instructor called,' he croaks.

'Did she? Why?'

'I'm not a fucking idiot,' Leonard says. 'Don't treat me like one.'

Years ago, if the brothers got into trouble, Leonard would slap them with the back of his hand. His knuckles, gravel-sharp, left deep bruises on their tender cheeks. He threw the brothers under cold showers, fully clothed, or locked them in the cupboard for hours on end.

'What did she say?' asks Jackson.

Leonard scrapes the last of the bubbling beans onto a plate.

'She tried to fine me. I said be my guest – I can't pay it. Not my fault if the kids went AWOL from your state-sponsored boot camp.'

Jackson carries his plate to the table. Frank taps a beat on the chequered plastic. 'You aren't mad?'

Leonard sighs. 'It's all politics, isn't it?' Everything is politics, according to Leonard. E-numbers. Adverts. Sea levels. Wars. 'A bunch of cynical careerists and incompetent backstabbers,' he snarls, lowering himself into his armchair, 'sitting smug in their ivory towers, carpet-bombing instructors with regulations, and now this bureaucratic nonsense? Honestly, the sodding state of this cunting country.'

They gather round the tiny table. Trapped steam haloes the TV screen, diffusing its twitching light.

Jackson feels strangely nervous about the absence of punishment. Leonard used to tower above them, but now he is shrunken, brittle-looking, his skin so thin it looks almost translucent. He eats less, coughs more. The ranting rage has faded, and in its absence a sulking resignation has taken hold. Jackson told Leonard to see the doctor. But Leonard has seen the doctors – all the doctors, too many to count. He had the scans, tests, operations, inspections, drips and drugs and drainings. He watched blood get sucked from his shrivelled veins. He shat in a plastic pot. What more does Jackson want?

'Ffanks for dinneh,' Frank utters through a mouth crammed with food.

'Frank,' says Jackson. 'Please.'

'*Sssshhhhhhhhh,*' Leonard hisses, jabbing a fork at the screen.

The newsreader sits beside a CGI graph: the red line plummets in a sawtoothed dive. Nonsense flashes on the bottom of the screen, ticker-tape strings of capital letters.

The camera cuts to a pre-recorded report of a giant, sun-struck building. Dazed people flow from the revolving doors. They carry cardboard boxes filled with rulers, mugs, photos, files.

'What are they doing?' Jackson asks.

'They got fired,' says Leonard.

'Why?' asks Frank.

'They broke the economy.'

Frank had no idea that you could break the economy. He doesn't really know what 'the economy' is, exactly. He pictures a massive, infinitely complex machine: a computer the size of a mountain, denser than a city, shinier than gold, composed of intricate networks of iridescent strings. 'What do you mean?'

'The banks got greedy and now they're fucked,' says Leonard, dropping his fork to the table. 'And so are we.'

On TV, the people walk away from the building, slightly aimless, lugging their boxes. 'They going somewhere?' Jackson asks.

'Yeah,' says Leonard. 'To hell.'

Jackson remembers the early years in Leonard's flat as a mixture of moods and confusions. Being in the flat felt like floating miles above the world, distant and superior, surveying the city spread below. At the same time, it felt like a dungeon, a prison, an underground cell. Some days the wind would barrel up the building's side. The brothers let their paper planes shoot like rockets at the moon, their glowing bull's eye. On calm nights they sent their planes sailing, spiralling, strafing through the cross-currents, and after their meandering fall they would land, many minutes later, on the car park below. It felt like sending messages, it felt like escape. Sometimes, Jackson remembered the flat was temporary. It brought him comfort. Other times he knew the opposite: that this was their life forever, this flat, this man, these walls, and this brought him comfort too. He couldn't work it out. Some nights, he would creep onto the balcony and stand amid the plants whose leaves were blue-black in the darkness. He would look across the city and watch the streetlamps glow like Chinese lanterns on a tide, and feel alone, and feel connected to everything. He would sleep there, curled up on the balcony's asphalt, dreaming of night winds and endless seas.

The brothers don't have a bedroom. They sleep in a tumble of squishy cushions, sagging duvets, and bed sheets piled on the living room floor. It's almost autumn, but the air is still warm, and so they leave the balcony door ajar. Fumes rise from the five-lane road. The city ticks and whirrs.

'We going back to the office tomorrow?' Frank whispers, kicking the duvet to make it dance.

'Not tomorrow,' says Jackson. 'Soon.'

It's time for the Dragon. Leonard lies pillow-propped in his bed, skin greyish in the light of the single bulb. His medicine box is like an advent calendar, a grid of miniature plastic chambers stuffed with an assortment of AM and PM pills. Leonard plucks a fat one from the box. Jackson watches the snake-like pulsing of Leonard's throat as he swallows.

'Where'd you go then?' Leonard asks. His eyes are half-closed, his voice creaking. 'You need to get better at lying. You don't even like football.'

The Dragon – Frank gave it the name – is a dark green box, connected via a hose to a transparent plastic mask. Before, Leonard used it when he had an attack. Now he uses it every night.

Jackson flicks the switch. A coal-red light comes on

and the Dragon whirrs.

'I panicked,' he confesses.

'That's why you have to prepare,' says Leonard, raising a finger. 'Otherwise they'll catch you. Didn't you listen? I thought we went through it all. This is basic stuff.'

'It's harder with you,' says Jackson. He tells Leonard about leaving the North District Institute that afternoon to visit the office he found. He explains it's not the first lesson, they've been doing it for a while, and Leonard nods quietly, eyes half-open, wheezing. Jackson reaches the end of the story.

Leonard says nothing.

'I thought you'd be mad,' Jackson says.

Leonard just shakes his head. Jackson places the mask over Leonard's mouth, which makes him look like a jet-fighter pilot. He breathes long, rattling breaths and the Dragon breathes with him, in and out, in and out, pushing the oxygen deep inside and pulling the bad air out. Leonard's asleep within moments. Jackson unclasps the mask from his face, tugs the duvet over his knees, and turns to leave. Leonard is already snoring. The shuddering glissando makes Jackson think of a bassoon, an instrument the brothers learned about on a science programme called *The Beauty of Mathematics*. The door shuts with a click. He turns to face the living room. Frank is asleep on the bedding on the floor, mouth agape, scribbled scraps of paper all over his chest.

III. A FLOATING HOME

Walking down the river path, Frank blinks towards the centre of town. Hot light slants from a restless sky, sheathing glass buildings in glare, reflecting off the tea-brown river to dazzle his eyes. The path teems with stressed-out commuters in sensible shoes. Leonard's coat swings at Jackson's shoulders, the black leather cracked like chapped skin. Frank scans the crowd as he walks. Most people's gazes are zombie-vacant, transfixed by their phones or thin air. Others glower at the morning with radiant scorn.

Summer came early this year. Miasmas of rubbish-gas hang over bins. Brown grass crisps in the heat. There are rumours of rains but they never arrive. The papers are already calling it the hottest summer on record.

The brothers pass an ice cream truck. Bloody slicks of strawberry syrup ooze down white ridges of ice cream. They walk on. Coffee vapour haunts the air. Frank inhales the morning. Beneath the river's brackish smell is something delicate and herbal, as though unseen flowers are blooming.

Stalled tourists squint at the river. An aster hangs high on a backdrop of clouds. The air throbs with the stuttering drone of its whirring blades. Frank should be used to the noise by now, but it always makes him nervous. Asters are meant to respond to riots, but Frank thinks they're what start them. That sound. It does something to crowds. A barge tugs tonnes of junk downstream. Frank feels a brief pang of inexplicable joy.

The brothers take a left and reach an underpass under the train line. Curved brick amplifies the roar of passing cars. Trapped fumes linger, itchy at the back of Frank's tonsils.

'I'm hungry,' he says.

'You're always hungry.'

'I mean it this time.'

They emerge into the shadow of a half-built tower. Bundles of steel beams swing, glinting weightlessly mid-air. Glass panes flash in the rising light. Frank fixes his gaze to the pavement. Fissures branch like lightning through the slabs. A stupid thought occurs to him. Watching a tower get built is like watching a tower explode, except in reverse, in slow motion. He pictures a city of buildings of glass spires collapsing, reforming, collapsing.

A playground jumps with ballistic kids who scream as they fight and play, crisscrossing the rainbowed tarmac. Two weeks into the summer holidays, the city's swimming pools are packed.

They head into a greenish patch of protected emptiness, ivy creeping up the walls. People in vests and straw hats kneel and make tea by a row of tents and airbeds under tarpaulin awnings. Others wash their hands in bowls of water. Hand-wrung clothes hang from a length of stretched twine. The brothers take a seat on a bench. Jackson breaks a flapjack and hands half to Frank. The sticky stodge reminds Frank of the honey toast Leonard cooked for pudding.

'Listen,' Jackson says, bringing Frank back to the garden. 'I've found something. Something important. It floats.'

'You're not going to tell me about your shits, are you?' Frank asks.

'Drag your mind out of the gutter,' says Jackson.

A pigeon struts in agitated pentagrams across the flagstone. The aster Frank saw earlier hangs in the morning, a fixed point, shredding the wind.

'It's a boat. A houseboat – one we can live in. It's just sitting there. No one's using it. We need somewhere to stay. So we take it. Simple as that.'

They walk towards the green. Jackson gestures at a stretch of blue hoarding at the far end of the road. A building has been partially demolished. Floor upon floor of flats stand gutted, wind rifling through the furniture. Yellowed wallpaper draped in peeling strips. Frayed sofas. Cracked basins. Tangled wires.

'How about there instead?' says Frank, grinning. 'Set up in one of those rooms. Breeze would be nice in this heat.'

A digger's toothed scoopers gnash the lip of a bathroom floor. A groan, a crack, and floorboards tumble: a sink breaks open, exhaling a cloud of pulverized plaster. Dust billows bright in the sun.

'Listen,' says Jackson, 'I know it sounds weird but I'm being serious.'

'I know,' says Frank. 'I'm just not sure what this is.'

Now and then, Frank and Jackson would return to Leonard's flat – or what was left of it. The block had stood empty for months, inert as a headstone against the sky. Leonard had fought a bitter, bloody-minded battle with the council, who had offered him a smaller flat in a different city, miles away from anyone he knew. Jackson told him to take it. Frank stood in the doorway, peered through the cracked-open door, and watched them talk: Leonard, skeletal and whisper-quiet, low in his armchair and wheezing the Dragon; Jackson, arms folded, shivery with anger, pleading with the stubborn old man.

The building, when they returned, was a strange thing to look at. Frank had grown up there, could remember no previous home, but now it had the look of a dead thing, an architectural corpse. Growing up, the courtyards and alleys echoed with bouncing balls, running feet, and skittering radios. The balconies were stuffed with plants, bikes, drying clothes. Flags billowed here and there, like sails, and made the building look, to Frank, like an enormous and ramshackle cruise ship, sailing tall and proud through the city. He believed for a while that all towers were boats anchored to the earth, which at any moment could uncouple from gravity and sail away, should their captains decide to depart. What else could explain all those blocks that vanished overnight, and all those shiny new towers that sailed in to replace them?

It happened slowly at first. The evenings grew eerily quiet. Fewer lights in the windows. Letters slid under doors. Court cases between tenants and landlords fizzled out in defeat for the former. Protests were quietly ignored. Families vanished, there one evening, gone the next. Men in hardhats and hi-vis waistcoats materialised, sealing the doors of freshly vacated flats with sheets of perforated metal. They cling-filmed the windows and poured concrete down the toilets.

None of it made sense. So Frank and Jackson developed a theory: residents were being taken off and slaughtered. The word 'decanting' started floating around. The brothers came to believe that this was a gruesome form of industrialised murder. They pictured people being herded into vans, driven to out-of-town facilities, where they were blitzed to soup in giant blenders and poured into vats of gore.

The parapet is barely higher than Frank's shin. He steps onto it and looks down. Sheer glass plummets beneath him, a wall of warped reflections doubling the street. Black stains of spat-out chewing gum dot the pavement. The distance bristles with cranes. Closer to, Frank glimpses unfinished structures of brick and steel, hollow shapes like excavated ruins or the skeletons of sunken galleons.

The air tastes singed. It must be laced with invisible dust, the atmosphere flooded with smog and scurf and powdered grit wafted up from sites all over the city, excavations, demolitions, endless pile-driving and digging unleashing clouds of particles like trees shedding pollen in spring, the dead cells of vanished structures migrating down the streets and into his nose, his lungs, where they seep into his bloodstream, the city warping his biology, concrete hardening bone.

He wanders down the parapet. The blocks beneath his feet are wide, but when he stretches out his arms he feels like a tightrope walker. One misstep and he'll fall.

'A boat is a floating piece of space,' Jackson declares, reading off his phone, 'a place without a place, that exists by itself, that is closed in on itself and... at the same time—'

Frank is fond of heights. He likes to climb cranes after dark and sit in the pods, pulling levers and pushing unresponsive buttons while he gazes over the amber grid, the lit channels of main roads and the bobbled black texture of public parks. Whenever he climbs a crane he reaches a point, roughly two thirds up, when the buildings fall away. It feels like bursting out of water and tasting air. He loves the freshness of cooler atmosphere, the wind on his cheeks, the horizon's clean unbroken line. He watches heaps of sand and stone and the tangled metal beneath him, the silver-black river's curved flank, countless points of light like a galaxy's stars, his stiff fingers gripping the rungs. Being up here, on the parapet's edge, feels like that, too. He is standing on the roof of the world: unseen, seeing everything. The world is a map.

'That doesn't make sense,' he says.

'It's Foucault. He says this thing about boats which is really—'

Frank zones out: he finds it dull and annoying when Jackson talks about theory. It makes him feel like he's at the Institute, which is not the point of these lessons. He makes a mental effort to blank out his brother's words.

Buses throb in the stalling traffic. Frank pulls a fistful of crap from his pocket: a crumpled ticket, a chunk of gum like a broken tooth. The wind tugs flecks of lint from his palm and he watches them float like dandelion seeds, swirling in the dust of demolished buildings.

Jackson looks up from his phone. 'You know what happens if you fall, right?'

'I'm familiar with gravity, yes,' says Frank.

A bead of sweat dribbles down his spine. Later this afternoon, the heat will reach that itchy, aggravating pitch that inspires drunk people to brawl.

'Is something going on today?' he asks, glimpsing hints of a distant park. 'A protest maybe?'

'Not that I know of,' says Jackson. 'Why?'

'No reason,' says Frank.

The roof is one of their favourite places. The faulty fire exit is easily opened from a back alley, and the stairwell leads straight up to the unlocked door. They've been coming here for months and only once got caught. Frank doesn't mind the risk. He likes the view. He can see for miles. North, towards the hills and the pylons. East, towards the estuary. South, towards the forests of cranes.

At night the brothers climb up with cans of beer. They lie on their backs with rucksacks for pillows. They stare at the blanket of zero stars as the sky-snakes unfurl in the eastern districts: shimmers of crimson and indigo as the factories blow waste-vapours into the breeze. The smoke is toxic. Everyone knows and nothing changes. In sheltered dwellings across the marshes, babies are born with no eyes, four arms, webbed toes, no legs, or so the rumours go. Someone told Frank that the colours are added to the gases, a hypnotic distraction from the damage they cause.

He remembers one particular night. The sky was a different colour because of the moon. Something to do with a shift in the atmosphere, which worked on the sky like a lens. The pitted orb was comically huge. It looked like it would crash into earth any moment.

'There are oceans on the moon,' said Frank, feeling recklessly sentimental and dizzily drunk.

'Fuck off,' Jackson replied.

'The Sea of Tranquillity. The Sea of Fecundity.'

'The Sea of Bullshit.'

'I'm serious!' said Frank, a chuckle sparking inside him. 'The Serpent Sea. The Sea of... Cold, I think.'

He remembers that night so clearly because of how strong and strange it felt to want to tell his brother he loved him. He wanted to say it as simply and as stupidly as that. It was embarrassing. He didn't care. He would tell his brother he loved him because one day they'd both be dead and maybe Jackson would never know. But the feeling failed to summon the words, so he said something stupid instead.

'One of them's called The Sea of Moisture.' He waited a moment, heart pounding. 'That's a fucking weird name for a sea.'

Jackson kept a wad of money in a box at the bottom of his rucksack, cash set aside from his decorating jobs. He blew his money on a bicycle, second-hand, picked up off some guy on a forum who swore he hadn't stolen the thing but was blatantly lying. Sprayed black, the bike had drop handlebars and old-style lever gears. The chain clicked and flickered as Jackson cycled, pedalling so hard the headlamps blurred as he overtook cars and trucks, wind screaming like a plane engine in his ears. Drivers honked as he veered across the lanes; they wound down their windows and hurled abuse until their faces turned puce with road-rage. Jackson didn't give a shit. He was moving through the city, a dizzy rush of limbs and gears. He had places to be.

Somewhere else. The phrase sang in his head as he cycled. Somewhere else. Somewhere else. Somewhere else. He was sick of here. This. These streets. These people. This sky. He wanted a world beyond it all. Beyond the pigeon-nibbled chicken bones and dirty curbs. Beyond the stop-start traffic lights and the pavements that teemed like virulent petri dishes. Beyond the dim scream of his nervous system, the endless pressure in his head. Somewhere else. He didn't know where it was – that was the point – but he knew how to look for it. He got lost. And when he was lost, he kept going.

It was late. He'd been cycling for hours and the city was deserted. He scanned the empty street, trying, and failing, to get his bearings.

He slowed to a crawl, tyres crackling like static on the rain-wet road, and glanced up at the bright signs of a handful of shops. A column of compacted flesh rotated slowly in a kebab shop window. Jackson considered asking the guy behind the counter what part of the city he'd strayed into, but then he realised that he didn't want to know. He felt like a kid again. Roaming the streets for no other reason than a hunger to run, to get lost. He turned left at the junction, peeled off down a twisting road. At the roundabout he took the darkest, narrowest turning, and his bike began to judder as the tarmac gave way to cobblestones. The long street curved past corrugated walls and wire-mesh fences. He saw brown brick structures, crumbling smokestacks, gleaming conjunctions of glass and steel. And then, to his right, the gaping entrance to a wasteland. An old and faded sign, daubed on a plank of wood by hand, was fixed to the wonky gate with a rusty screw: *Ever wondered what happens when you die?*, it read. *Trespass here and find out!*

After locking his bike to a drainpipe, he heaved himself over the wall. The gravel expanse held a strange glow in the darkness, as if its surface was dusted with pulverised moonlight. Squat plants jutted through the sheet of powdered rock, and black tyres were stacked in towers amidst the stiff, twisted fronds. When Jackson reached the far end of the clearing, he tasted water on the air. It was a creek. The muddy banks gleamed beneath the amber of the streetlamps, lamps he could not see directly but whose glow was reflected and diffused by the pollution that hung above the city like the dome of a cathedral. A silver trail ran down the centre of the channel, flowing towards the river, the gaping estuary, the sea. Footprints littered across the mud, tiny asterisks left by wandering birds. Reeds bristled against the brick, black rubber, and iron, while the far bank, now he looked closer, was clotted with broken wood, and draped with capes of algae. How had he never been here before? This tiny, twisting creek had escaped Jackson's meticulous mapping.

It was late but he wasn't tired. He went exploring, wandering down the skinny ledge that ran alongside the banks. The cold rising off the mud was pungent. It smelled somehow nutritious, laced with minerals, vitamins, and other strange, good things, despite the copper-salt tang of rotting seaweed.

He saw the boat a short while later. Something about the angle at which it rested, not quite flush with the wall, intrigued him. He had passed other boats already, barges with protruding ribs and rotten boards, boats with busted hulls and gaping sides. But this particular boat looked different, promising, and oddly familiar, like a face he dimly remembered but could not put a name to. As he edged towards the boat, step by slow step down the wall, Jackson was overcome by the sensation that he was walking towards his own death. By stepping into the lightless void of the boat's interior, he would enter a kind of Hades: a dark inversion of the city he hated and loved, around which he would drift like a pale, forgotten thing, a shadow of a shadow of a shadow. He liked the idea of oblivion. If this boat was his tomb, so what? Nothingness would be a relief. The padlock on the wheelhouse door came loose with a quick smack, and he stepped into the dark.

For a moment, there was nothing. No light. No sound. Then, steadily, his senses adjusted.

Pale light sifted through slits in the curtains, falling in pools on the speckled carpet. The air was thick with a fug of mildew and mould. He held his breath and listened. The sound of the water rushing past the boat echoed the pulsing of blood in his veins, the ceaseless tides within his body. Breathing again, he inspected the rooms at the back of the boat, grim little cabins with squishy-looking mattresses he half expected to find corpses lying in, their leathery skin stretched loose over cages of bone. Back in the main room, he opened the stove. Its metal chamber was dusted with ash. He scrunched up an old receipt and lit it with his lighter, watched it curl and burn and cast a brief, amber light on the floor.

The flames sank and finally died: darkness flooded the room. The boat had changed somehow; it felt different, every particle strangely charged. He saw what it would look like in daylight, clean and fixed and sailing smoothly. The night was cold but his blood was burning. He stood in the wheelhouse as the dark water flowed and saw it lead him away from here, out of the city.

They cycle to the derelict stretches of the city's southeast. Frank has never been here before. It feels like a different city, a grey maze of empty yards and anonymous warehouses. The pavements are pale and strangely clean, as if freshly unwrapped from the package. The boxy trains on the overpass drive themselves. An old brick bridge stretches over fenced yards and a clutter of buildings, low and stooped beneath sheet-metal roofs. In a row of garages and wrecking yards, mechanics prowl round the gnarled hulks of crashed cars. An LED screen flashes red and blue above the door of Mount Ararat Ministries, garish against the rain-washed paint:

THE END OF ALL FLESH IS COME
BEFORE ME FOR THE EARTH IS FILLED
WITH VIOLENCE

The brothers have been cycling for over an hour, rucksacks knocking on their spines. Frank is sticky with sweat all over. Chests heaving, they take turns with a plastic bottle.

'Don't backwash,' Jackson says.

'Fuck off,' Frank replies, grinning. He lifts the bottle to chug the last gulps and kicks dust at his brother.

They cycle down the road that curves off to a playground. Three young women spin on the merry-go-round, passing a joint back and forth. At the churchyard they take a sharp left, a right, left again, then straight down a cobbled street, past an abandoned café and a hand-wash garage. Bored workers are playing dominoes.

Frank detects a new smell as they move, a breath of salt and silt. A path leads off towards a bridge. The brothers walk down it and lock up their bikes.

Low tide in the creek. Rugs of emerald moss are draped on the mud. Heavy, brown-brick wharves huddle round the banks and machinery looms in the dust-spooked windows. A mouse darts over the wall, swift and silent as the shadow of a bird. Frank can hear the rush of traffic, the whir of the aster's blades, but they are quieter than the sounds of the creek: the rush of water and the drip-dripping of moss.

'How did you find this place?' he asks.

'I went for a walk,' Jackson shrugs, a sly grin on his face.

Old boats litter the mud. Frank casts his eye across the discarded things, as useless as the wrecked and rusting cars he glimpsed in the MOT depots earlier.

The brothers make sure not to slip on the stretches of algae that interrupt the thin path. Moisture thickens the humid air, more of a mist than a rain. The creek bends right as they walk, curving as the water curves to open new views. Patches of flourishing buddleia burst through the brick walls on the opposite bank. Jackson slows to a halt.

When he sees what his brother is pointing at, Frank's mouth flops open. 'Are you kidding?' he gasps.

It looks like a gnarled lump of coral, scorched and peeling, swelling from the stinking mud.

'Needs a bit of work,' says Jackson. 'Nothing we can't handle.'

'It's a ruin.'

'Cosmetic,' says Jackson. 'Trust me.'

He steps on to the roof of the boat and unlocks the padlock in the wheelhouse door. Frank has no idea how his brother does it. He works ten-hour days painting walls, and spends hours each night on his bike, doing Frank doesn't know what, before crashing in the bedsit for a couple of hours and starting over again.

Frank steps aboard. The paint is flaked and rusty, but the barge feels as solid as stone.

'What is it about the words "trust me" that make me immediately suspicious of a person?' he asks.

'Cynicism,' Jackson replies.

Frank grips the railing and leans overboard. The curved front of the barge is bearded with algae. Its lower regions are skirted with silt. He stares at the rusty hole from which an anchor might have dangled.

Frank holds his tongue. He hasn't seen inside the boat yet. Maybe something awesome is lurking in this destitute shell. Maybe it marks the entrance to an underground lair, a hidden system of subterranean caves and thundering waterfalls. Why else would Jackson bother? The boat is a piece of shit. The rain-swollen wood of the wheelhouse has the porous look of wet bread.

Frank daydreams about swimming in cool, clear water as he stares at the banks of dull mud.

He follows Jackson into the wheelhouse. The space is occupied by a slanted panel inset with buttons, levers, keyholes, and dials, with a giant wooden wheel in the centre.

This, at least, is something.

Frank grips the wheel. He pictures himself as the captain, guiding the boat through mountains of thrashing water, or through the starry depths of outer space as celestial squid fly past. He bashes coloured buttons at random, but the wheel won't budge. It annoys him. He grips a handle and yanks with all his strength. A grinding sound shudders in the bowels of the boat.

'Shit – did I break it?'

Jackson laughs.

They step through the door in the back of the wheelhouse and into the main cabin. Patches of mildew blacken the walls. Moss has grown between window and frame. Beige fronds spill from the guts of a torn cushion. There's a tiny kitchen to the right, furniture in the middle, and an iron stove at the far end. Frank blinks in the dimness, shifting his weight from foot to foot. The blue suede curtains dampen the light.

'Couldn't we just find a flat,' he says, 'or a warehouse or something? Someplace dry? This boat is... disgusting,' he says, pretending to choke on the air.

Jackson stares at the stove. Fresh wood is piled beside it and crumbly ashes are heaped on the grate.

'It's about what it could become,' he says. 'It's about picturing something insane, and then actually doing it.'

Jackson is in one of his abstract moods. He leads Frank to the room in the back of the boat. A bed is wedged against the curved wall, pillows dim in the portholes' light. Frank peers at the words and the pictures. Maps, drawings, photographs, charts, photocopied pages and handwritten quotes are pinned collage-like to the walls. There's a blurry photograph of their mother on the shingle in the blue night under the moon, a nuclear power station far away in sloped dark. He sees some of his own drawings, too. Like the portrait of himself as a monkey god. He hasn't seen the drawing in ages. He had no idea Jackson had kept it.

Being in this room makes Frank feel as if he's been sucked into Jackson's head. There are confessional notes, diary entries, which Frank feels too embarrassed to read. There are maps and attempts at drawing. Hand-copied quotations from the essays Jackson argues about with strangers online. This boat, this visit, is not some spur-of-the-moment thing. Frank is here for a reason. There's a dark spark in the back of Jackson's eyes that Frank hasn't seen since they lived with Leonard.

Jackson has assembled a makeshift desk from the door of a kitchen cabinet and two low stools. At the cen-tre is a cardboard model of the boat, beads of dried glue gleaming at the joins. The tiny rooms are kitted out with model furniture. Circles the size of bottle caps are cut in the cardboard walls. Frank peers through them at the matchbox sofa and fights the urge to laugh. He rarely feels protective of his brother. But this model is so tiny, so fragile, that he begins to confuse it with Jackson, who seems equally vulnerable here.

A huge map of the country dominates the main wall. Jackson has embellished it with a network of blue lines. They branch like veins across the map.

'Canals,' says Jackson. 'Old pathways. Hardly anyone uses them now. They'll take us wherever we want.'

Frank follows the looping lines with his finger. He's only been out of the city a couple of times. He went on a trip once with the District Institute, years ago, to a youth hostel, where they rambled round ruined castles and scooped pearls of gelatinous frogspawn into glass jars, waiting for them to hatch. But the only world he's ever known is the one he grew up in. Tarmac. Sirens. Pollen. Towers. The thought of leaving fills him with a confu-sion of excitement and dread, a sense of anticipation that borders on fear. Jackson's text said: something to show you, meet me at 8. No further explanation; no sense of destination or aim.

There is work to do, painting and clearing. The brothers get dressed in paint-spattered shorts and T-shirts. It's still too hot. Frank peels his top off and opens the windows, opens the doors. The breeze is feeble but better than nothing. Slowly, the tide fills the creek. Soon it is sliding calmly past the boat with a faint glassy sound. An old radio rests in the corner. It has a telescopic antenna and a horizontal dial. Broadcasts wrestle for frequency. Speed garage collides with hip-hop and dissolves into static, interrupted by billows of grainy opera. Frank fiddles with the dial. He feels that if he found the right frequency, he could tune into Jackson's thoughts. Instead he finds local talk radio and pirate stations. He knows he is looking for something. A stray voice in an ocean of noise.

Frank goes slowly snow-blind, pushing, pulling the paint-soaked roller, eyes fixed on the whitening walls. He should be bored but he isn't. It's oddly fun to measure time by distance instead of duration, counting the hours by the square-metre, watching the work progress. The sound of the rollers calms him. But he is Frank. His mind wanders, gets lost in the woods. Soon his concentration slackens completely. He gibbers nonsense and stares at his toes.

'*Arrk arrk arrrrrrrrrkk,*' he squawks, flapping his arms. He stops. 'Hey Jackson.'

'What?'

'It *is* kind of like an ark, isn't it?'

Jackson claps his hands to get rid of the dust. 'You need a break,' he says.

They perch on the wall and watch a swan glide down the water. The bird is such a clean, bright white, and moves with such grace through this landscape of mud and rust that Frank believes it is a mythical creature, a minor god in animal form. Frank had no idea how hungry he was until now. He wolfs down fistfuls of bread, biscuits, crisps. After lunch he lies back and rests his head on a tuft of weed. His lids glow purplish red in the sun. Frank's feelings have changed since this morning. Maybe Jackson is right. The barge is both a weapon and a refuge. It isn't just a vehicle: it's a key to unlock geography.

Frank sits up from his half-snooze and yawns. Sunlight stuns the water; it takes a moment for his eyes to adjust. The heat is so intense Frank can hear it. That wilting sound. That sizzle.

'Water?' Jackson asks, passing Frank the bottle.

Frank swallows a mouthful of lukewarm, plastic-tainted water. He hasn't felt this close to Jackson in months. Not talking. Not needing to talk. Doing stuff together: that's all.

Later that afternoon, the brothers climb down to the mud with a pair of spades. Jackson hands Frank a pot of gloss and instructs him to paint the name of the boat on the prow, to christen their floating home. Frank considers this for a moment, but really it could only be one name. He paints the capitals slanting across the prow: *ARKADY*.

The tide is low but not fully out. Ankle deep in the mud, they dig around the bottom of the barge. It has been here for so long that, even at high tide, when the water laps almost as high as the portholes, it stays glued to the creek bed.

They dig for about an hour. A moat appears around the edge of the boat, slowly filling with water. It deepens, but the barge doesn't move. So the brothers dig deeper, spade after spade.

Without warning, a mudbank collapses. The boat springs forward with a sharp crunch. Frank dives sideways just in time. The barge almost crushed his legs. He fumbles and slips like an injured seal. Jackson hasn't noticed Frank's face-plant. He's too excited about the barge. It has slipped. It will float. They are free.

'Excuse me!' Frank says. 'A little help?'

'Look at that,' says Jackson, hands on hips. 'Beautiful.'

'I'm trapped,' Frank yells. 'Trapped!'

Jackson, finally noticing Frank, grabs his hand and pulls him upright. A thick, pasty layer of stinking clay clings to Frank's body. He sputters and spits, shakes his arms.

Jackson guides Frank by the elbow, ankles squelching in the mud. The tide is not fully out. Further down there is a bend in the creek where the water slows and pools. It is astonishingly clear. Frank can see the algae-slicked stones and gravel, chunks of reddish brick and emerald weed. A school of tiny fish dart at his shadow. He peels off his clothes to his boxers and lowers into the water. Stunned by the heat, he lies still, eyes closed, as water flows across his body. Jackson lifts handfuls of water and pours them over Frank's chest and legs. Frank kneels and submerges his head. Soon all the mud has gone. The water is deliciously cool. He stands up and stares at his wet, pale hands. They sparkle like sand in the sun.

The brothers are hungry and tired. At dusk, once the sky turns powder-blue with ragged gashes of ember-red, they cycle northwest in search of food. A swarm of black asters hangs low in the sky, haunting the streets with the roar of their blades. People walk briskly, gripping their bags to their chests. Figures zoom on mopeds down the streets. Blackvest vans skip red lights. Teenagers stand in groups on street corners, swigging beers, smoking, laughing, listening to tunes. Frank wants to hang out and get drunk, but Jackson is pedalling hard already, sloping right to overtake a lumbering truck. Frank quickens his pace to keep up.

The brothers stop for food in a chip shop. Jackson's phone died a few hours ago; he plugs it into the wall at the table near the stuttering light. They eat fish and chips in silence. Frank goes heavy on the salt and mayo. He watches figures move down the darkling street through the ghost reflection of the room in the glass. Jackson's phone buzzes and jumps on the plastic top.

A flat screen is perched on the drinks fridge: BREAKING. The footage is shot from above, revealing an isometric view of the city, a thin crowd gathered at a cordon. Black smoke billows through the dusk, a vertical column slanted by wind. Flames roar from blackened windows and creep up supports. Rumours have been flying round for months now: there will be soldiers at train stations, tanks on the streets, but so far they haven't appeared. Perhaps this is it, Frank wonders.

Jackson taps and swipes his phone. His eyes are lit blue by the screen.

'What's going on?' Frank asks.

'I don't know,' Jackson says, 'but people are saying it wasn't the rioters.'

The brothers wipe their Styrofoam boxes with their last salt-dusted chips and wash them down with tap water. On the screen, the camera cuts to a close up of masked figures leaping over fences as blackvests give chase.

'Told you something was happening,' says Frank. 'On

the roof, remember? You—'

'My phone was dead. People have been messaging me all morning.'

'About what?'

'Everything. It's kicking off. Some kind of march is going on nearby... Too much to follow, confusing... But one thing people keep saying, even the news.'

'What?' Frank asks.

'Two people are dead.'

The owner wearily nods at the flatscreen and tells the brothers he's closing early. Jackson's phone is at thirty per cent. They head back outside. Shadows gather in the trees of the park. Invisible asters thrum above, search-lights swinging through the night. The streetlamps diffuse a strange glare on the streets as the brothers ride. Frank wants to go home, wherever home is: Jackson's cramped pay-per-week bedsit, maybe, or back to the boat. His muscles ache, his eyes twitch. He is desperate for sleep. Jackson steers his bike with one hand, taps his phone with the other, checking notifications and maps. The streets are quiet for a moment. Frank could com-plain about the long day, his exhaustion. He could admit to feeling scared about where they are headed. But his brother would never listen. For the next ten minutes, hot wind in his face, Jackson barely looks up from his phone.

Slanted windows glow turquoise. Their pale light con-jures shadow-puppets on the brick walls of the buildings nearby. The brothers lock their bikes and climb onto the warehouse roofs round the back of the high street, from where they can watch the march without being seen. Frank leaps across the luminous panes. The glass could crack and swallow him in a shower of glinting blades, but he knows how to listen for weakness underfoot. His ears attune to the rattled music of the building as he runs: the click-clack thud of fat bolts jumping in their holes, the creaky whinge of the sheet metal bending. Buildings sing to him in moments like this. A wrong step could be the difference between living and not.

The brothers pause by a chimneystack overlooking the street. Frank rests his palm on the brick. A fire exit runs down to the alley; the alley leads onto the street. Whatever they saw on the news is only part of the story. Protestors have gathered outside a blackvest station – a couple of hundred, Frank would guess.

'Why are we here?' he asks.

'Go home if you want,' says Jackson. 'I don't care.'

The crowd stirs outside the station. Kettledrums pulse at the heart of the march. A lit flare arcs overhead and the street burns crimson. It snaps off a double-decker and cartwheels over the street. Red smoke swells from a sputtering flame and drifts across an agitated crowd. The protest is muddled, unfocused. Placards show politicians' faces photoshopped with bullet-holes and bloodstained hands; others, hand-painted on cardboard, curse the brutality of privatised police. A banner has been hung across a shop front – PEOPLE not PROFIT – the capitals picked out in black. But the corner of the banner is torn, the plastic sheeting frayed to shreds, swastikas scrawled in felt tip in the centre of each O.

A smoke grenade hisses nearby, thickening the air with eruptions of lilac. Lamps darken and distance dissolves. Frank can barely count the fingers of his hands as they walk.

A rangy guy in a boiler suit drifts into the brothers' path. Smoke clings to the cricket bat in his hand, elastic strands like molten marshmallow. He wears a scarf over his mouth, his high forehead shiny with sweat. A young woman follows close behind, her face obscured by a gas mask that makes her look insectile, alien. Frank catches a flash of dark eyes in the circular lenses before she melts into smoke.

His mouth hangs open. The air tastes like burnt caramel, acrid and sweet. He turns to face his brother, but instead of seeing Jackson, there is a whirl of red smoke.

Frank shouts his brother's name in a mouse-squeak voice. The street is too loud and too quiet: everyone is shouting, but the thick smoke muffles the sound. Frank jogs in random starts and spurts, bumping into strangers. Shadows swim through the smoke. Disembodied heads and limbs leap into view before dissolving just as quickly. So many faces, so many cliques and crowds, but Jackson has disappeared. Frank coughs up a mouthful of something that tastes like blood.

Another double-decker looms. Parked awry on the kerb, its windows are scrawled with spray-paint glyphs and symbols. Head down, eyes up, Frank scurries towards it. Blue trucks' engines throb nearby. Drums thump a slow, hypnotic rhythm at the heart of the march. A firework roars towards an aster overhead. It explodes in a willow of amber sparks that momentarily brighten the street.

Frank curses his brother. The longer they spend here the higher the chance they'll be kettled with hundreds of restless protestors, or hauled to an off-the-grid detention centre in the shadow of train lines and power stations. The thought of returning to one of those places fills Frank with dread. Strip-lights flicker in the cold grey room. You go for hours without food or water. Why risk it? He isn't sure what the point of the protest is, what it could ever achieve.

He stumbles on a clearing. Pink smoke swirls in billowing walls around the hazed edges, but the tarmac stage is empty and still. Torn leaflets stir among smashed placards in the heat. It is strangely calm in this pocket of air, like the eye of a storm. Bodies move behind the smoke, shadows swimming in coloured air. He indulges in a familiar daydream: that this is the moment his mother will return. She will walk out of the smoke, a wise smile on her face, stand in the clearing, and hold out her hand. I was lost. I was joking. I'm back.

A giant stomps into the clearing. Ten feet tall, it staggers and howls. Slack limbs flail either side of its segmented torso. Dumbstruck, Frank stares at the monster and crouches, ready to run.

The monster is two young men, one perched on the other's shoulders, both yelling at the top of their lungs.

Another firework pops above them, a sudden pulse of light beneath the aster's anxious churn. Frank crouches, squinting for a route of escape, but the light keeps shifting, the smoke grows thicker, and his ears ache with the stampeding drums. Someone lights another flare and for a moment the world burns crimson, every surface ablaze. A rubber bullet smacks the man clean off the other's shoulders. They topple like a felled tree, throwing sparks as they crash.

Smoke shoots into his eyes. The air darkens to dusky purple. He splutters and gasps for oxygen, pawing his way through a substance so thick it feels viscous. A hand shoots out and grips his arm. His panicked feet stutter; he falls.

Grit bites Frank's palm where he lands. He expects to see his brother's outstretched arm. Instead he sees the outline of Arkady, the man who haunts his dreams about drowning. Arkady's head looms in the burning haze, inscrutable, featureless, dark. His black-gloved hand reaches out to pull Frank upright, to pull him elsewhere, into a different city, perhaps. Arkady says nothing. The world is silent.

The smoke thins. Frank's senses come back into focus. Arkady's features shrink and solidify.

Dark eyes peer through the black mask's circular lenses. It's the young woman Frank spotted earlier – she was prowling behind the man with the cricket bat. Now she is yanking his arm.

'Frank?' she yells, voice muffled by the mask. 'You are Frank, right? Jackson's this way.'

Frank is too stunned to argue. He follows her through the protestors and the smoke begins to clear. An empty space stretches between the blackvests and the rioters, tarmac glittering with broken bottles and pocked with scorch-marks. Wheelie bins lie toppled, trash spilling from open lids, and looted shopfronts gape. Smashed windows lie in screes across the pavements, splintering the light from a burning car spewing smoke through a missing windshield. Graffiti crawls over the spider-webbed glass, spray-paint dripping: KILL PIGS.

'This way,' says the woman, and she points at an alley.

Frank sees Jackson standing there, peering into the crowd.

But things are happening all around him. A heartbeat later, a shopping trolley heaves into view, wheels squealing, weighed down with rags. They set the rags alight and push the flaming chariot through the front of a fabric shop. Within minutes, the shop is ablaze. The street out front burns amber; the sky darkens under a pall of smoke. The headache stench of burning rubber drifts down the street. A moment later, the blackvests, who'd been keeping their distance up til now, begin to march.

Their armour plating shimmers in the heat-haze.

The path between Frank and Jackson is blocked by obstacles and rushing bodies. Weaponry lines the street, lethal lengths of wood and metal poles, broken bottles with serrated jaws. The shop is blazing fiercely, pirouettes of black smoke whirling madly down the road. Frank hefts a chunk of brick. It misses the blackvests by miles, popping to dust where it smacks the pavement. Blackvests drive though the protestors' ranks.

A thrown bottle ricochets off Frank's skull, shoots over the tarmac and whacks off a curb, spinning like a Catherine wheel beside a burning banner. He veers sideways, firelight dancing in his eyes, a clear, high sound in the air like the ringing of a faraway bell.

By the time Frank reaches Jackson, the blackvests have surrounded the protest. The brothers are crushed into the space between the bank and the van, the windows of the shop fronts cracking under the impact of lengths of scaffolding swung by protestors in head-to-toe black. Frank recognises one of them from the cricket bat he holds in his hand, the skull-scarf pulled over his mouth. The young woman with the gas mask gestures desperately at him, but he shakes his head and turns.

'Where the fuck did you go?' Jackson shouts. He clips Frank round the cheek. The impact stings a little, but the adrenaline in his system numbs the pain.

'Come on then,' the woman yells, a new edge of desperation to her voice. 'The way out. Where is it?'

They push through the crowd, hand-in-hand as they duck through the smoke. Frank keeps an eye on the chimneystack. Soon they reach their escape: the shadowed alley, the roughness of brick, the cold relief of metal stairs leading up to the roof.

The marshes murmur with insects kindled to life by the

dark. Fireflies sway over channels of water that branch through beds of reeds, twisted, tangled streams in whose dull waters lurk fat fish. Frank lifts his nose to the wayward wind. It carries a fragrance of burning wood and the fermented stench of marsh-mud. Sleepless factories stand nearby, chrome flues leaking neon into throbbing pools. He scratches the back of his neck and glances up at the shivering sky.

'I'm starving,' he says.

He isn't particularly hungry, but the silence has begun to unnerve him.

Lali crouches in the dirt, twisting blades of grass around her fingers and methodically ripping them apart. Her gas mask rests beside her, a shed skin or a second face, its hollow discs facing the sky.

'Don't have any food,' she says. 'It was a protest, not a picnic. Isn't there stuff on your boat?'

'We only just got it today,' Frank says, feeling slightly dizzy from the beer.

Lali rocks on her heels.

Frank has been watching the path for what feels like hours. Sometimes headlights comb the marsh and turn the reeds to glowing filaments. A car will park for a moment, engine on, and drive away a short while later. Motorbikes stutter down the path, headlights jolted by divots and ruts, the canal water flashing like a blade.

Earlier, the three of them had slipped like cats across the roof and dropped into the streets beyond. Endorphins barrelling through their blood, nerves lit up like Christmas trees, they'd bent double in breathless laughter, cackling under the headlamps and coughing up lungfuls of smoke. Then, once the giggles faded, they'd headed back to the boat – Lali limping; she'd done something to her ankle landing from the roof

– and started guzzling cans of beer, the alcohol a balm to frayed tempers. Lali didn't drink. She was agitated. She needed to go; she'd lost her friends, who weren't answering texts or calls; they'd agreed to meet at some hut in the marshes, a location agreed in advance. Jackson said they'd take her in the boat. He didn't ask Frank what he thought, just checked a map: it wasn't far. Maybe Jackson was drunk, or just showing off, but in moments the engine was running, and Frank ran outside to watch the water churn white as they set off.

'It's just you two, then? You and your brother?'

The question is so direct, the answer so obvious, that for a moment Frank just gawps.

Lali stands upright and narrows her eyes. She is as tall as Frank, and just as skinny, but her poise is faintly menacing, as though she might slit his throat with a practiced flash of her arm. He'd seen it in the protest: the feral quickness with which she moved. Now that her mask is off, Frank can see her fox-like eyes, freckled cheeks, and the short boyish cut of her hair.

'Who else would there be?' he asks.

'Comrades,' she says, her tone flat, as though the answer was obvious.

The word is unfamiliar to Frank, but he nods sagely, clenching his jaw to convey his authority, experience, and understanding. He wishes his brother would return. Jackson elected to roam the dark marshes in search of the hut, volunteering after Lali's bad ankle got twisted in a ditch.

'You were there because of the Citadel's mail-out, right?' she asks. 'I didn't see you at the demonstration. Just after, when things got messy. Who told you it was happening?'

Frank shrugs.

'Wait – you weren't there on purpose?'

'No.'

'You've never heard of the Citadel? The Red Citadel?'

'We do stuff,' Frank shrugs, defensive, wishing Lali would shut up. 'We go out. We don't get involved. Sometimes it gets involved with us. We didn't have to help you out, but we did.'

'It was a protest,' Lali snaps, 'with political aims. Do you even know what it was for, what we wanted to achieve?'

Frank shakes his head. She throws her hands up and sighs.

'What's the Citadel?' Frank asks. He pictures an obsidian fortress surrounded by crackling storm clouds.

'It's a place,' says Lali, 'a long way north. They've been fighting the state for months. They organised the protest tonight.'

Frank doesn't quite understand, but nods as though he does.

Time passes slowly out here, away from the quickening heat of the city centre. The minutes creep and stall. He listens to the rustle of life in the marshes' dark, wild animals, insects, birds, and sees himself as a hunter, spear in hand, stalking the flat, wet land for deer. Then the factory catches his eye. If any deer lived on this land they'd be warped mutants with radioactive antlers and poisoned blood. He could try and catch a fish but it would probably give him cancer.

A strip of tarmac, cracked by weeds, stretches towards the canal; at its far end a gutted bi-plane rests lopsided on broken landing gear. Overcome by tiredness, Frank kneels on the dirt. Stiff reeds chatter softly. Fireflies drift over inky pools.

He spots a shadow moving through the reeds. The

shadow raises its hand.

'That's him,' says Frank. 'I think he found it.'

They walk along the canal path. Beyond the foaming weir and the hunchbacked trees, beyond the whispering grasses and the lights of the other houseboats moored by the lock, is a haze of light. The city's electricity seeps into the purple-dark sky. The horizon is lit by constellations of crane lights and interrupted by silhouettes: spires, obelisks, slanted wedges of construction.

Frank had expected a grotty hovel, a tumbledown hut built from maggoty boards. Instead it is a clean, new outhouse, freshly painted lilac blue, adjoining what looks like a holiday home: a two-storey cottage with a front garden and a thatched roof. People have gathered in the garden round the back around a small fire on a gravelled area seemingly built for that purpose. Maybe a dozen people are seated around it, chatting: their voices quieten slightly at the sight of the new arrivals. Several of the group were clearly at the protest. They wear dark hoodies, black jeans, and carry rucksacks adorned with red patches. A twisted yew tree grows nearby, the scarred bark of its bent trunk underlit by flames. Other camps further off in the marshes have also lit fires. There are smoky smears of reddish glow, soft heat on a blue-black field.

'You found it!' Lali beams.

Jackson says nothing, just grins like an idiot. Frank hasn't seen his brother act like this in years, all floppy and eager to please, but he is tired and the marshes have chilled him, and he is eager to sit by the fire. He sits cross-legged at the edge of the gravel, half-listening as people talk about other protests, other riots, other cities: a country-wide uprising, a people's revolt. Jackson is nearby, swigging rum from a hipflask and laughing. He

settles his head on a folded jumper and peers at the sky.
A satellite moves across it like a red lamp on a zip wire,
a lone light tracing the dark.

IV. THE RED CITADEL

Kids from the Citadel kneel on a blue tarpaulin, armed with brushes, scissors, tape, and glue. They add the last flourishing touches to handmade placards, poster-paint houses with triangular roofs, stick-children weeping on crayoned lawns. Most of them are camo-patterned with spots of paint, faces slathered with finger-smears and daubs. Two boys wield placards like axes: they clash and tumble on the grass. Adults unravel banners, pull on baggy sloganed T-shirts, stuff leaflets into rucksacks, and fill flasks with steaming coffee and tea. There must be a hundred people outside already, and more are filtering through the gate. He watched the luggage pile up in the lobby last night, bin bags bulging with duvets, pillows, rugs, and clothes, hand-washed in the communal kitchen and hung to dry in the tin-roofed warehouse.

Two young men and a woman, older than Frank, drift past in torn jeans and battered caps. He asks for a light. The young woman's black hair is shaved on one side, long on the other, sleek fringe swept like a raven's wing over her forehead. She digs a Clipper from her jeans. Frank lights up and wishes he hadn't. Smoke clings to his teeth like oil. He stifles a gag.

'Do you live here?' she asks. 'Are you, like, *involved*?'

Frank nods. He declines to mention that he doesn't actually live here, just shares a barge with his brother nearby.

The woman shakes a cigarette out of the pack. 'What's it been like?' she asks. 'I've been meaning to come down for ages. I keep reading about you guys online, but then...' Her sentence trails off with the smoke she exhales.

The guy with the glasses scowls. 'It's disgusting what they're doing.'

'We're still here,' Frank says, glancing at a restless

blur on the horizon. The buzzsaw humming is so constant these days he barely hears it anymore, but there they are, in the rain-shivered sky: a trio of asters.

Plywood walls encircle the Citadel's grounds, their royal blue paint rain-faded and graffiti-scrawled. The walls are tall and lend this patch of oil-soaked earth the feel of a city-state, a fortress of safety, walled against the outer world. The earth is lush with straggled carpets of overgrown weeds, most of which Nell cultivated. There are bristling strands of rhubarb-pink knotweed, their virulent roots spreading under the soil. Kudzu froths in great waves over hangars and crumbled walls. Narrow paths run from the padlocked gate, past the satellite huts and studios, and to the Citadel's yard.

The woman with the black hair stamps: 'Exactly. I'll handcuff myself to the gate if I have to.'

'Wow,' says the guy in the glasses.

The path that runs past the canal is fringed on one side by bursts of buddleia. A handful of barges are moored beneath the flyover that curves overhead on fat stilts. Pot plants dot the barges' roofs and lamps glow in the windows. At night, wood-smoke drifts from the chimneys. Ivy embroiders the flyover's stilts. Tents and shacks have spread in the shadows. It feels different from the city Frank grew up in, colder, smaller, easier to navigate.

There are cities within the city. Unofficial districts have appeared in public parks and empty yards. Dwellings, assembled from scraps of fabric, metal, wood and wire, hunker and lean against brick walls and mesh fences. Plywood shacks spring up in a matter of minutes, bashed together with gaffa and nails: the rickety mansions collapse under heavy rain and are repaired within hours. Tents flourish overnight like nocturnal flowers, dusted with the exhaust of passing cars until the colours fade like someone turning down the saturation.

Frank and Jackson would see them on cycle rides and rambling walks. Tents at the edge of a green. Mattresses down an alley like beds on a hospital ward. A woman cooking food on a camping stove whilst kids played in the duvet-lined boot of her car. Lives were spilling out of buildings and flooding the streets. The Citadel was not the only occupation of its kind. Since winter, evicted families and rent-hike casualties have been living in empty flats, offices, garages. The crackdown was rapid. Blackvests flew from building to building, emptying occupations, arresting people by the busload. Only the Citadel is left. The High Court letter arrived a week ago; they'll be here first thing tomorrow.

He steps into the wheelhouse and opens the door on the interior gloom. Jackson isn't here – he left for work early this morning, long before Frank dredged himself from sleep – but something compels Frank to sit for a moment and wait. He rests on the steps in the dimness and breathes the comfy singed odour of ash from last night's fire.

The city changed after the protest, after the meeting by the marsh. Its physical texture altered – the fences, bollards and spikes, the security kiosks that appeared on street corners, the council blocks that were blown up in controlled explosions and quivered to heaps of rubble – and so too did the way it felt, adjustments to mood which were harder to measure. The protest had been small but it was part of a chain reaction. The city erupted. Protests divided, multiplied, and catalysed into riots; riots triggered counter-protests and crackdowns. Blackvests began patrolling the streets, armies of sala-ried guards protecting the patchwork of private spaces the city had become. The brothers were afraid of what the city was becoming, day by grinding day – but they had the boat. The freedom *Arkady* afforded, its embodiment of escape, felt, in the definitive light of departure, unexpectedly sad. So Jackson hatched a simple plan: they would cross the country in search of the Citadel.

For weeks they travelled aimlessly, guiding their route afresh each day, surviving off a dwindling pile of cash. Soon they were halfway across the country, a world of unfamiliar accents, bad weather, and impossible skies. They worked as they travelled, gutting the interior, stripping and painting the walls, fixing the hinges of broken doors, and scavenging furniture, bedding, supplies, to fill the space and make it liveable.

Eventually they reached the outer limits of a city smaller than the one they'd known, but which, like the place they had left, was built around a river. Its wide waters were green-black in the evening's dark. The brothers, exhausted, guided the boat through a network of narrow canals and locks until they reached the place Lali had described. It looked like nothing. A strip of blue hoarding; a narrow path edging the canal; and, on the opposite bank, a flyover booming with cars at this late hour. They followed the hoarding round until they reached a gate. The Citadel stood on a huge plot of brownfield land. Frank was tired and cranky; he shouted at Jackson, said they'd reached the wrong place: the grounds were dead when they entered. Weeds surrounded them, untamed. The place was as hushed as a greenhouse, the humidity thickened with a late-summer fragrance of blooming and rot. Frank followed Jackson through crumbling buildings and rusted hangars, grumbling, kicking stones. Jackson was wrong. This wasn't the place. Then his vision shifted. Signs of habitation began to emerge: lit windows, clotheslines limp between walls. Through gaps in the weeds they glimpsed a giant, hulking building, a crude cube clad in red metal. He saw figures outlined by a flickering bonfire. Since then, the brothers have stayed here: moored to the canal round the corner, visiting the Citadel often but keeping to its fringes.

Frank snaps himself out of his daydream. He calls out Jackson's name but it's clear from the clicking quiet that the boat is empty. He checks his phone but he needn't have bothered: the screen is blank.

Nell's shuttered door is open onto the cluttered space of her studio. Shelves heave with pot plants, canvases, and ceramic figurines shaped with her fingers and thumbs: harlequins gleaming with craquelured glaze. Frank flinches the moment he sees her, shields his eyes. Sparks flow from the joint in two lengths of steel, the stuttering light reflected in her letterbox visor. She turns off the welding torch and lifts the mask on her broad, striking face set with pond-green eyes.

'Frank,' she nods. 'Morning.'

There is a wide patch of floor in the studio's depths, which is cluttered with strange shapes. There are metal spheres with flexible tubes trailing out of their sides. Spidery cradles of welded steel. A spiked ball like a naval mine. Nell scours the canals and backstreets for discarded things, from which she assembles these dream-logic sculptures. Frank is puzzled by her art, which she hasn't exhibited in years; he can't tell if it's great or shit, but he knows it makes him feel a certain way.

'Thanks for coming. I could use your help with something.'

Nell moved into the old warehouse twelve years ago. She turned it into a studio and has been living here ever since. A short walk south, on a strip of brownfield, was the building that would later be named the Red Citadel: a giant commercial facility, a red-walled warren of windowless cells. An anthropomorphic cardboard box grinned over the driveway. The logo's still there today, its toothy grin faded by rain.

The building in whose shadow she lived was a self-storage block, a temple to consumer stupidity. It absorbed the leaked excess of people's homes, the sofas they bought but didn't need, the crass lamps gifted by tasteless relatives, the exercise bikes they tricked themselves into thinking they'd one day use for cardio. Five years ago, Pendragon had bought a handful of plots – the land around Nell's warehouse, the storage facility and a cluster of satellite buildings and brownfield swathes surrounding it – off the council, for a third of its worth. They emptied the buildings, most of which were already disused and tumbledown, and let the land lie fallow. Weeds dislodged the cobbles, wild things nested under spiderwebbed roofs, concrete cracked, disintegrated – and all the while the land crept up in value, month by month, as foreign money speculated on new developments, glass-and-steel ziggurats, gilded towers. Cramped, tight, lightless, the facility's room's were stuffed with forgotten furniture, juxtapositions of tacky lamps and lumpy armchairs, bags of clothes and rusting bicycles: a glut of discarded things that intensified the residents' contempt for the city they felt had robbed them.

A group of activists, Nell among them, crowbarred the windows and changed the locks, turning the cell-like rooms into a network of rudimentary bedrooms. They drilled holes in the sheet-metal walls for ventilation; begged, borrowed, and stole bedding; and nailed pages of legal terminology to the front gates, talismans against eviction.

'It's a sty,' she says, ushering Frank inside. 'Can't be helped. Or: can be helped. I can't be bothered.'

'Would be pointless anyway,' says Frank. 'You'll be in jail this time tomorrow.'

Nell throws her head back and cackles, grey threads flashing in her hair.

Bare-brick walls support a distant ceiling. At the far end, a ladder leads up to a wooden mezzanine with a mattress in the middle, bookshelves on the wall, clothes' racks hung with coats and shirts. Beneath it is a basic kitchen: a sink and an oven hooked up to an orange gas canister. A long worktable runs down the length of the room, its surface scarred and stained. On it are a notebook, a mug, a glass jar with a paintbrush jutting out of its milky fluid, and a litter of papers: court documents, official letters, leaflets and posters and placards. Frank skim-reads the letter at the top of the pile, which arrived a few days ago and has been circulated among the residents:

YOU ARE HEREBY NOTIFIED that effective 7 DAYS from the date of service...

surrender possession...

fail to do so, legal proceedings will be Instituted against...

on which date, having secured a WARRANT FOR POSSESSION from the High Court...

'There isn't a time on here,' says Frank, 'just tomorrow's date. How do you know when they'll come?'

Nell looks up from the kettle. 'They always arrive at the crack of dawn. Maximum rudeness. Salt in the wound.'

'They could come any time, though, right? Like four or three or six or—'

'Thank you, Frank. I am familiar with the concept of time.'

They sit on a wrought iron bench in the garden out back of Nell's studio. The lawn is fringed with wild bushes with purple, black, and white flowers. A few of Nell's works are displayed here: glass bells mounted on metal blocks; an intricate iron-rod structure hung with mirrors that flash as they twist in the breeze.

Frank inspects his tea. Fragments of green stuff swim to the surface; others lurk in the depths of mug. 'You said tea,' he says, 'not lawn trimmings.'

'Green tea,' Nell says. 'It's obscenely good for you. L-Thiamine. Antioxidants.'

'Anti-whats?'

Music drifts from the Citadel's radio, a swelling symphony, rich in cellos and horns, that warbles over the hubbub of the gathering crowd. A stray cat appears on the grass and picks his way towards a patch of sun, his tilted ears attuned to the murmurous building. Volunteers, led by Nell, have divided the land into allotments dotted with planters. Blue-green cabbages glisten with rain. Marrows fatten on yellowing vines. A scarecrow stands awry in a wither of brambles. On its face is a joke-shop Prime Minister mask, the pendulous, hollow-eyed face staring blind at the dirt.

'Are you worried about tonight?' Nell asks, peering at the quickening clouds.

'Isn't everyone?' Frank replies. 'The mood in the yard is... weird. All these strangers milling about.'

Evil-looking plants jut from the clay pot at her feet. Tight bunches of spiky, reddish heads are clustered round crazed clusters of roots. She started planting the Japanese Knotweed months ago, as deep as she could bury it, a virulent plant that would outlast the residents,

111

a rebel weed that would crackle and creep through the buried foundations: a form of biological sabotage to lower the value of the land.

'I guess it's different for you and Jackson. At least those people are here for a reason. You don't know if you're staying or leaving.'

A dumb bee, drunk on pollen, staggers through the grass at Frank's feet.

'None of the options are good,' he says. 'Even if we win somehow, and we won't, it won't make any difference in the long run. What would victory even look like? Arthur thinks we have a chance of beating them, but that's Arthur, he's completely insane. You should have seen him at the gate. He was bashing a can with a crowbar.'

'Surely not,' says Nell, in a grimace of mock-surprise.

Arthur was one of the first to arrive at the Citadel. He formed the Committee with Nell, a group of activists who took possession of the old block and turned it into ad-hoc social housing.

Soon the whole building was filled. The waiting list grew by the day.

The brothers refused a room, preferring to live as the Citadel's satellite. Moored to the canal nearby, they spend much of their time in the grounds, doing favours and scrounging hot meals, drinking beers and fixing rooms. But they've always felt like, or wanted to feel like, outsiders. Vulnerability was the root of authentic belonging, but vulnerable was a feeling or a state they struggled bitterly to avoid. Since they were never in need of the Citadel (they had the boat), they never truly belonged there (they could always leave). And unlike the anarchists, the Trotskyists, the anarcho-communists, the socialists and the socialist workers, the Sisters, the

Blues, the Bohemians, all the other splintered, bickering factions who'd moved into the building, they never saw the Citadel as an opportunity to advance an agenda.

Jackson had taken Frank to places like this a few times before, but the Citadel felt different. The group who started it – Nell, Arthur, Lali, Caspar – called it an 'occupation': to others it was a 'brazen, Robin Hood attempt to redistribute wealth' (the local paper); a 'grim hovel of spoilt snowflakes and whiny troublemakers' (a government spokesperson); a 'cynical, pointless scam' (Pendragon, the multinational developer who owned the land).

An energy flowed down the Citadel's concrete corridors, under the glare of industrial lamps. Heat moved through the metal-walled rooms: an indignant belief that they were the good guys, the government and the developers bad. The world was fucked up, needed fixing, and they were the ones to do it. Frank guzzled it up. That unstable concoction of frustration and despair intoxicated him.

'There's no way the city will change,' he says, 'because no one knows what change looks like. We've never seen it, not out there. We can only make it happen in miniature.'

'I wouldn't call this miniature,' says Nell. 'We've helped hundreds of people. Thousands are watching the videos.'

'And what does it actually change?'

Nell shrugs. 'Opinion.'

'If voting made a difference they'd have made it illegal,' says Frank.

'Who fed you that one? Caspar? Think about the people who'd be on the streets without this place – who will be on the streets tomorrow.'

They drift towards the garden's end. Grass fizzles out to a dirt path that runs round an orchard of crab-apple trees.

It wasn't always a garden. The dirt beneath their feet has gathered over decades, sifted from the sky, compacted to mulch in the wake of dead industry. Only hardy plants survive here, roots delving through soil studded with buried coal. To the east is a dry, wide barren pool of dust, a dumping ground for the factories' chemicals. It's a miracle anything grows here, according to Nell, who keeps a book of pressed flowers, stalky specimens of rabbit-fur brown and powder blue.

Frank plucks a lump of coal from the dirt and hurls it at a nearby tree.

'To make things better you need to know what better looks like, right?' he says. 'But everything's confused. There's no centre.' He peers at the Citadel, where a group of activists are attaching a black banner to the roof: people not profit. 'Arthur wants to make noise and piss people off for no real reason. Caspar's itching to start an anarchist revolution. Lali wants to go viral. Marco wants to make a fucking documentary. All the new arrivals are protest tourists. There's nothing higher. Nothing shared.'

'We're a collective. Of course it's messy – that's almost the point. What do you want? What does Jackson want? You're here but you're not here. You come and you go.'

Frank observes the sky. High winds carve the cliffs of vapour, shearing the mountainous clouds into steeper angles.

'It changes,' he says. 'First he thought it was us alone against the world, and that the only way to live how we wanted to live was to shut everyone out, y'know... To protect each other. Be disciplined, insular, like a cell. He wanted a revolution. I guess he thought revolution began at home – that if you got things right between two people, that was a model for how a whole world might work. Then we met Lali.'

'And she brainwashed him?'

'I never said—'

'I was joking. He's very strong-minded. I'm sure she just... pointed him in a direction.'

'It seemed like maybe we weren't alone. But we're working things out still. Everyone is.'

'I get that,' says Nell. 'It wasn't an accusation.'

'And he's not as aloof as you think. He was with you at court.'

Nell had organised a demonstration at the district court building, where the Citadel's committee had gone to fight Pendragon's Warrant for Possession. Frank had stayed at the Citadel to guard the building against the lifters. He watched the marchers return at dusk. Fewer than fifty were left. Those that returned moved slowly, heads bowed, bedraggled and drained. They carried tatty placards as they streamed down the cobbled street.

During the day, whilst the crowd outside the courthouse waited for the verdict, and whilst the Citadel Committee made their arguments to the judge, the street became a miniature festival. Music throbbed from a bass-bin. Faces were painted: lions, tigers, blazing suns. Protestors climbed trees to hang bright banners and flags from the branches. A table, strategically manned by the cutest kids, offered leaflets and cups of tea. News filtered out of the airless courtroom. The crowd's mood plummeted; the carnival soured. People in costumes and face paint stood with hunched shoulders, wobbly tears in their eyes. The DJ killed the music. A banner slid off a tree-branch, pooled in a heap in the gutter; a moment later, a bus crushed it under its wheels.

Frank had rushed down the path to greet the returning marchers. None paid him any attention. They walked in silence through the Citadel's grounds and slouched on logs and plastic seats around the fire pit. Jackson, finally, appeared. There was a gash on his cheek, a red swipe clouded by mauve. The shoulder of his raincoat was torn.

'What happened to you?' Frank asked.

'Nothing,' Jackson replied.

'Nothing has a strong right hook.'

They halted at the rim of the fire pit. Fragments of dead leaf glistened on rain-wet charcoal.

'Aren't you going to tell me?' Frank asked. 'Everyone's drifting along like a zombie.'

'We lost,' said Jackson. 'That's it. End of. The eviction will happen. No appeal.'

The lobby was strewn with paints, paper, glitter, and scraps of card. The colours, so bright that morning, were pale in the murk of the unlit room.

In the kitchen, Jackson cracked open a can and gulped. Lit by the cold of the open fridge, his face was wan and slack, and the scratch on his cheek lurid red. Frank fetched the first aid kit from under the sink. He unzipped the green fabric satchel and offered it to his brother: antiseptic, sheaf of plasters, roll of gauze.

Jackson sneered. 'I'm fine,' he said, gulping another mouthful of beer. 'Just got trampled.'

'Trampled? Who gets *trampled*? Did a load of wildebeest turn up and—'

'One of us fell over. Went to help them up. Tripped. Cheek got wedged against a brick,' he said, pointing. 'What are you smirking at?'

116

The Citadel's garden faces southwest: it caught the last of the day's fading light. The sun cast long shadows over the soil and the tangled growths in the allotments, vegetables that would, in time, be ripped up, bulldozed, pulverised to baby food. Frank glanced at the scarecrow as they stepped into the cool air. Lit from behind, the empty eyes of the Prime Minister mask glowed red.

A stage has been erected near the fire pit: a knackered platform of wooden crates, topped with plywood sheets, with a painted banner backdrop. Mizzle sifts from the sky. The air is effervescent. One of the Citadel's residents sets up a stool and a mic-stand on the improvised stage and shuffles off a moment later, ankle tangled in a stray audio wire.

'There are so many people,' says Frank.

Even compared with the court date, when dozens of strangers gathered to march, the Citadel's yard has the crushed stressful feel of a major station at rush hour. Bodies criss-cross and paths overlap. Nearby is the trio Frank saw this morning, perched in a ring near the beetle-bright trailer, munching salads from tupperware boxes and scrolling on their phones. There are nervous young people in hesitant clutches hovering by doors or walking tight circles in the gardens nearby. There are strident kids who scream and laugh, oblivious to their parents' angst; teenagers cross-legged on the dirt, arguing over online articles; a topless man, perched on an oil drum, slapping bongos; and people gathered beneath the awning, milling, like bus stop tourists, waiting for a sign.

And then, beyond the crowd, are Caspar's friends.

They appeared in a van last week, a bunch of six young men.

At first Frank thought they might be brothers.

They shared Caspar's hunted physique: those striated, long-distance-runner's limbs, that sunken look in their scheming eyes. Today, like every day, they all wear monochrome. Black jeans ripped at the knee; black coats stitched with shouty patches; black fisherman's waistcoats, pockets loaded with who-knows-what. They move like foxes. Scrawny, mean.

The wall is Arthur's bright idea. Built from junk and salvaged scrap, he thinks it will keep the fuckers out – even though, as several people have pointed out, there's already a wall around the whole plot of brownfield: a ten-foot hoarding and a buffer of outhouses. Will a layer of heaped junk make a difference? Nell called it a waste of time and energy, an exercise in posturing. Almost everyone agreed. There was a vote. Hands were raised. When Arthur comfortably lost, he shrugged, and said he was doing it anyway.

Caspar's friends are keen technicians. Side-by-side they slot junk into the trench. Kitchen doors and broken furniture. Mattresses buckled on chests of drawers. One of them – slightly stockier than the others, with a sculpted beard – hauls a red plastic jug as he walks, slopping gulps of greasy fluid into the trench.

'Come,' says Nell.

She guides him through the double doors. The frames are rust-red like the building's front, the panels fogged with scratches.

'I want you to talk at the meeting,' says Nell. 'If we ever get there, that is.'

'Talk how?' Frank asks. 'I don't have anything to say.'

'Ask questions,' says Nell. 'Agree. Disagree. Just... talk, okay? Open your mouth.'

The crowded reception is sauna-hot. Leaflets, banners and placards are stacked in towers. In the corner, a young woman shields the windows with a patchwork of baking trays, gaffa tape, and newspaper pages that muddy the light. A group of young protestors whom Frank doesn't recognise are testing handcuffs on the staircase railings.

'Do they fit?' one asks.

'Your wrists are too fat, man. No offence.'

Frank is used to the reception. He often spends time here in the mornings before lessons and lectures; he'll sometimes set up a chair in the corner to read. In the mornings, there is coffee and talk as people ready themselves for work; in the afternoons there are workshops, exercise classes, art therapy for kids. Today the space feels chaotically different. Isolated, aimless groups jostle at the curved front desk, under the absurd watchful gaze of the storage company's logo.

Nell steps over the protestor slouching on the stairs, whose wrists are now chained to the railings: 'Haven't you got jobs to go to?'

The young woman chained to the railings laughs.

They reach the creaking blue door at the top of the stairs. Frank follows Nell down the strip-lit, identical corridors lined with identical doors, a stutter of interior tunnels that shudder with a colourless light. Footsteps shiver down the corridors, tight echoes bouncing off the bare metal walls. Now that eviction is imminent, the building feels like a place of departure. Now and then they pass an open door. The rooms' floors are littered with things left behind by vanished residents: molehills of clothes, pillows and sheets; a photo of a beach hut tacked to a wall; power cables snaking over rugs and sleeping bags.

They pass rooms in which people are gathered, packing rucksacks and saying goodbyes. Frank glimpses other preparations through open doors: a spot-lit table on which glass bottles are laid; a smoke-filled room with a circle of stools; a load of saws, hammers, and crowbars scattered on dunes of sawdust.

'Wait,' says Frank, feeling dizzy, twisting his head so the corridors spin.

Nell glances back. He's reached a crossroads or a junction, a point where corridors overlap.

'I'll meet you upstairs,' he says. 'I won't be late.'

He jogs beneath the bleachlight of fluorescent tubes. Numbers flicker as he goes. Sound carries oddly in the Citadel, partitioned into near-identical rooms whose walls are so thin you can hear people breathe next door: the corridors fizz with echoes and whispery voices. Eventually he reaches Lali's door, which is closed. He stands for a moment listening, raps his knuckles against the blue.

'Yes?' she yells. 'I'm busy.' He knocks again; she opens the door a fraction. 'Oh,' she says, 'it's you.'

Her tiny cluttered room is piled with clothes, suitcases, books, and bags. Perched on the flocked blue skin of her deflated mattress is her laptop, the window open on several self-replenishing feeds; in the corner is a battered armchair salvaged from one of the unclaimed rooms. She is packing her stuff up, preparing for tonight. The eviction is hours away. She will be banging the drum on social media, tapping into her contacts, spreading the word.

Frank finds her gaze disconcerting: she never seems to blink. 'You coming to the meeting?' he asks.

'Yeah,' she says, sounding distracted. 'Help me pack, will you?'

The room is roughly the size of a shipping container. There is space for a single bed and not much else; the

120

walls are unadorned, except for a few bluetacked photographs and a screenprint poster of the Citadel. She asks Frank to help pack her bag with clothes on the foot of the bed. Abruptly, it makes him feel awkward, unsure of his clunky hands: folding the T-shirts in which she sleeps, packing her knickers and bras. The room's trapped air sustains odours. Incense has burned here recently: a perfume of scorched dust floats.

Lali lowers her phone and fixes Frank with her levelling stare.

'You're staying at the Citadel tonight,' she says. In typical Lali fashion, this is not an enquiry but a statement of fact. 'Since this morning there are plenty of rooms.'

'Maybe,' Frank says, folding his arms. 'I'll have to ask Jackson,' he says, and, although he feels the truth of it, the words sound faintly pathetic. 'It's fucking pointless,' he snaps, 'isn't it?'

Shrugging into her raincoat, Lali shoots Frank another sharp look. The small room amplifies her presence, concentrates her gaze: Frank is struck by the sense that he's being held in this room against his will.

'Since when were you so *cynical*?' Lali asks, leaning back again, shaking her head. 'You're too young to be this jaded. You should fight. Otherwise you're just... I don't know,' she shrugs. 'Giving up. Giving into hate when you could make use of its opposite.'

'There's nothing to love about this city,'

'God, you're such a pointless contrarian,' Lali replies. 'You're worse than Jackson.'

'I paired your socks for you,' says Frank, grabbing a T-shirt off the top of the pile. 'Don't I get a thank you?'

Lali pauses to write a message, fingers scurrying over the screen.

'Love isn't just a squishy word,' she says, not looking

up at Frank. 'It has real political power. What else do you call what we're doing here? If people like you got up and *did* something about it, we wouldn't be in this shit. We wouldn't have apathy. We'd have—'

A quick report of knuckles sends a shudder down the metal door. Without waiting Caspar strides in, so tall he must duck to avoid the lintel. His head is scrappy with brownish hair. His Adam's apple juts obscenely from his sinewy throat; watching him swallow makes Frank feel sick.

'Oh,' he says, clocking Frank.

Frank is still holding Lali's T-shirt. He looks down at the T-shirt, up at Caspar, down again.

Caspar nods at Frank but looks at Lali. 'Is he—'

'Helping me pack,' says Lali, leaning over to drop a dry kiss on Caspar's lips. He closes his eyes; she doesn't: they separate. 'What's up?'

Behind him stand a pair of Caspar-clones, the black-clad skinny figures Frank spotted earlier, building Arthur's wall. They mumble to each other in the corridor. The taller one stops talking when he sees Frank.

'We should go,' says Caspar, enveloping Lali's shoulders in a skinny arm, squashing her face into his earwiggish torso. 'The meeting's about to start.'

The meeting, in fact, has already begun. There is barely any room left; the rooftop is swollen with plants and crowds. People sit cross-legged on the floor or perch on oil drums and stools, staring at Marco, who holds the stage. Frank hovers with Lali at the edge of the audience. He sees a few faces he knows. Caspar stands by the fire exit, scowling.

Seated, legs crossed on the plywood bench, Marco traces a shape in the air with his finger.

'We travel in circles,' he announces. 'We walk and we

walk. There are cogs in our bodies and cogs in the world. Constant motion, round and round. Portals open. The window shifts.'

Chunky lenses magnify Marco's eyes. His blue shirt hangs limp off hunched shoulders, collar loose round his neck. He has always looked to Frank like a turtle, wizened and stooped. There is a ripple of amusement at his words.

'We are the pebble,' says Marco, 'the city's our pond. Be the wingbeat that triggers the hurricane.'

Puddles have formed on the Citadel's roof. They mirror the rosemary, lavender, potatoes, and kale, the fronds withered in the smog and in need of nourishing sunshine.

'Tonight we can open the future,' says Marco. 'Believe it. Embrace it. Open that door,' he says. With closed eyes, gently, he rests his hand on his heart.

There is a smattering of light applause and many bemused expressions. Marco bows stiffly and shuffles offstage, leaning on his cane for support. He walks with a lilt that makes his camera swing round his neck with each step. He grins at no one in particular.

'He sounded stoned,' Frank hisses, clapping his hands.

'Don't be rude,' says Lali. 'He's probably just had one too many peppermint teas.'

These meetings are usually held in the reception downstairs, or, when it's warm, in the yard out the front. Frank has been to a few and he finds them intensely boring. First is the mind-numbing subject matter, the rotas, schedules, resident updates, and interminable lists of repairs. Second is the non-hierarchical approach. No one takes a lead. People can talk for as long as they want. The meetings usually collapse into quagmires of interminable back-and-forth tedium. But today, Nell appears to be in charge.

She steps onto the low stage and taps the microphone. A brief buzz of feedback squalls in the air. 'Brothers and sisters, comrades, friends,' she begins – her standard opener, a nervous glint in her eye.

'We have called our Citadel home for just over a year. We've achieved so much in that short time. Think how much we could change in another year. But that isn't how Pendragon see it.'

The crowd erupts into hisses and boos. Nell nods slowly, sadly, an ironic upturn to her lips.

'They call us spongers, scroungers, criminals. They intimidate us, they harass us – but why?' Someone shouts evil, another shouts money. 'What are they so afraid of? Democracy? Equality? Justice?'

Nell's words wash over Frank. He has heard this speech, in various guises, before, and finds himself tuning out. He scans faces, seeking out new ones. He tracks the movement of birds in the sky. Half an ear is cocked to Nell's words.

Things felt different the night they arrived. Lali introduced them to the other residents. Strangers called them comrade; they greeted the brothers like long-lost friends. They ate stew, drank wine, and talked for hours about how the city was changing: bad new government, streets on fire. The news was awash with aster-cam footage of tanks on blockaded streets, of candlelit vigils at community halls, of the homeless roaming the streets in droves. Arriving at the Citadel had felt like reaching the top of a mountain, everything suddenly clear. The world was a landscape of stark opposition, of moral continents. On one long and whiskey-addled night, Caspar told the brothers all about Pendragon, the company who owned the land on which the Citadel stood. They were just one serpent-head of the hydra of neo-liberal greed, a metastatic network of subsidiaries, sub-subsidiaries, contractors, and shell companies owned by a cabal of crooked billionaires and exiled oligarchs, who funnelled profits from oil and war and exploitation through warrens of offshore shell companies, and were based in a smoked-glass campus with a legal department more populous than most small towns. They were the Citadel's arch-enemy – and for a few weeks the story made sense.

People have begun to argue, cross-talking on the roof.

'They'll come at us with everything,' Caspar yells. 'Police. Blackvests. Cannons. Mace. Truncheons. Trucks. Lie down and it'll be slaughter.'

'No one is going to die,' says Marco.

'People are dying every day,' Lali replies. 'Innocent people, murdered by the state, and you're here giving us this mindfulness guru bullshit. If people want change they fight for it.'

Arthur – who has lain in a deck chair till now, leather coat pooled around him, chain-smoking unfiltered rollies and sipping a breakfast beer – calls for an all-or-nothing kamikaze battle, a carnival of communal violence.

'How many policemen does it take to push an innocent man down the stairs?' he asks, harsh voice cracking across the crowd. 'None. He fell.'

His asthmatic cackle shudders through the air.

Nell counters with a plea for peace. She wants non-violent resistance. A human chain.

'Arthur has a point,' Lali yells. 'Literally hundreds of people have died after police contact in the last five years. Guess how many convictions there have been?'

'Zero,' shouts a stranger, raising their fist at the sky.

The clarity is ugly and abrupt, like being woken from a dream.

Frank doesn't want to be here.

He wants his brother; he wants to leave.

Marco attempts to tune a guitar. People yell at him to be quiet.

Nell takes to the microphone to call for quiet. 'If we can – please – if we can just – listen to each other – listen –'

Light rigs mounted on the tops of vans throw long, sharp shadows on the dust. Raindrops flash as they needle the glare. Jackson arrived in a rush a few moments ago to find the street lit up like a film set, blackvests and lifters gathered outside. Further off, double-decker buses wait to haul protestors to detention cells. Cameramen aim their lenses at the Citadel's gate. Presenters in suits clutch microphones, wires coiling into their ears. Jackson doubles back on himself. He cycles along the plywood wall and along the canal. *Arkady* is dark. His phone is dead. He calls Frank's name. No answer.

Over the plywood wall, the high fronds of the knotweed thickets, and the curved bulk of the nearest hangar, searchlights swing through the Citadel's grounds. The asters' blades beat in time with his heart as he hauls himself over the wall. Rubble slips and tumbles underfoot. He hacks his way through a thicket of brambles. Soon he reaches the Citadel's entrance, dust ablaze in the light from the vans.

The chain-link gate has been patchworked with sheet metal, steel rods. Razor wire curls along the top edge. Sheets of screwed and bolted scrapmetal howl as the blackvests pound it with their battering rams. A head appears above the gate and yells through a megaphone:

'We hereby assert authority to repossess the following property or properties. Failure to comply with this order in a reasonable, peaceful and timely manner will be considered under Common Law as a Breach of the—'

Arthur wears a dinked tin helmet over bug-eye flying goggles. Black epaulettes adorn the shoulders of his camouflage coat. Jackson recognises the clothes; Arthur found them in one of the storage rooms upstairs. 'Shove your poxy jargon up your arseholes and fuck off back where you came from.'

Dark shapes slide like eels from the banks of knotweed. They gather in shoals near the gate, hoods up, faces masked in shadow. Fat chains drape in swags around their necks and limbs, links glinting like scales as they twist in the lamps. A group sits cross-legged on the earth, arms threaded into plastic tubes. Others handcuff themselves to iron drains and throw the keys into the rain-pummelled dark.

'Trespassers must immediately quit the property,' the voice rings out. 'Failure to do so will constitute a breach of the—'

The battering begins again, a heart-attack trill of irregular beats. Bolts and hinges rattle in the gate.

'Dude!'

Jackson recoils at the voice beside him. A guy in huge sunglasses and a pea-coat is seated in the lotus position, bare feet slimed with mud and rain. 'Get involved – I got a load more here.' He gestures to his open rucksack. A coiled chain gleams in the depths of the bag. 'Quick, yeah – they'll be through in a second, we've got—'

The front gate buckles with a wrenching howl. Patchworked metal groans beneath the wheels of a reinforced van; as soon as the gate falls forward the blackvests and lifters start streaming in, dozens of them, sheathed in dark grey boilersuits or shiny plastic armour. Jackson finds a narrow gap in Arthur's wall and crawls through, hands and knees dirty, feeling like vermin. His trousers snag and rip against the twisted head of an exposed screw. He's sure that Frank is nearby, but when he reaches the wall's far side and looks up at the smouldering, spot-lit roof, all he sees are silhouettes.

A figure lurches from the shadows: bushy beard, thick glasses, darting eyes.

'Marco,' Jackson says, voice ragged in his throat, 'where's Frank?'

Marco holds a camera to his chest, its glossy lens like a crow's black eye. 'Don't know,' he says, 'but you should see this footage, man.'

He flips the camera's window and plays a clip. There's a smear of fire and rushing feet, of flowers and plastic barrels, then the lens levels on a figure on the corner of the roof, leaning with one foot forward, the Citadel spread out beneath him, bright lights blurred beyond the limit of the lens's focus. He sparks a flare, lifts the sputtering fire above his head. The screen burns scarlet, soaked in red, skeins of thick smoke flooding into the air above his raised fist.

'Have you seen my brother?' Jackson asks, exasperated.

Marco gazes in the gate's direction. Spotlights whiten his lenses as they swing. 'Last time I saw him was on the roof,' says Marco. 'You'll need to use the fire exit. Front door's barricaded. Look.'

The Citadel's front doors, like the gate and Arthur's wall, have been reinforced using scraps and fragments. A fat steel pole is threaded through the handles of the doors. Shopping trolleys and bulky chests of drawers are piled up against the glass. A pair of bodies slump on the ground outside. Then Jackson sees the chains threaded round the handles, the handcuffs at their wrists.

Metal drums are filled with fires that blaze and crackle in the slanting rain. Bouquets of blackened wood spit ember-plumes and gusts of smoke and an oily reek of petrol stains the air. Jackson picks his way past leaf-heaped planters, glass bottles, and stacks of bricks, scanning the smoke for his brother. He checks his phone again. The screen is an infuriating blankness specked with rain – he fights the urge to smash it on the floor. He strides to the roof's edge and looks at the yard. Lifters breach the wall, clawing and pawing the scrap with gloved hands. They reach the chained protestors. Cries ring out.

'Where's Marco?' someone yells. 'Is he getting this?'

Jackson should never have left. He was weak and confused; it was stupid to go; he should have realised that the only important thing was Frank, the boat, their one way out. Now he is here in the roar of the night, watching Arthur prowl through the darkness below.

Arthur lights a flare and hurls it, the hot tip burning an arc. His goggles have gone but he still has his helmet and crowbar. Face creased in an impish grin, he screams at a phalanx of blackvests as they move down the path.

Caspar's friends pull shards of burning wood from the fires with charred barbecue tongs. They drop the flaming splints off the side of the roof, through a rushing tilt of rain: the fragments flicker on the wet mud far below. Another group of lifters prowl towards the Citadel, white helmets gleaming like teeth in the jaw of the dark. Vague figures emerge from the undergrowth, clods and clots of bodies, darkly clothed, like shadows in human form. Grouped together, they block the lifters' path and seal the gap in Arthur's wall with their bodies.

A lifter stands before a protestor, tilts his head at her;

words are exchanged. It's hard to tell in the rain but she appears to spit in the lifter's face. A scuffle breaks out, a tangle of limbs and chains and tugged wet clothing, jumpers twisting inside out, long hair flaring, truncheons raised. A walkie-talkie crackles at Caspar's waist. 'There were dogs. German Shepherds. A whole truck of them, barking.' Vans roll slowly down the path. The windshields, protected by metal cages, hide the drivers from view. Water cannons squat like limpets on the roofs. Caspar takes a run and chucks a wine bottle towards them, flinging it hard, overarm, like a javelin. It lances through the air and bursts to powder where it lands, a brief dry pop at a lifter's feet.

'Jackson,' yells Caspar. 'Where the fuck have you been?' His cheeks are gaunt, his forearms swimming with tattoos, his fingernails sceptred with dirt, his swagger cruel and streetwise, but he can't hide that private-school accent, that luxurious inflection in the vowels. 'Pick something up. What are you – a tourist?'

He presses a bottle into Jackson's hand. A grubby rag sprouts from its mouth; the inside, through the brownish glass, is filled with murky fluid.

'Fuck this,' Jackson yells. 'Where's Frank? Have you seen him?'

Caspar shrugs: 'Sure, he was here just now – used my phone.'

Lali's told Jackson things about Caspar's life that he'd rather not know. Like how Caspar's rich father, estranged, is a prominent politician; how he steeped himself in anarchist philosophies in a redbrick university. Details gather round Caspar's scrawny, vulpine head, a constellation of things to detest. Jackson says nothing.

'Everything according to plan,' says Caspar, firelight dancing in his eyes. 'You seen the cameras? Look up.

130

Asters in the sky. Two for the state, one for us – not that anyone trusts the TV – but listen, fuck it – we promised a show.'

He's on something. Not coke, which fucks with his ethics, but a dark-web upper of some kind. He grins, twitches. His huge dark pupils swallow light.

Jackson asks Caspar about Frank again and doesn't bother to hide the desperation. Caspar shrugs. He says sure. Frank was here a while ago and was asking for Jackson; he borrowed Caspar's phone and tried to call but the line was dead. Maybe Lali knows; maybe Nell. Caspar has other things to do: he turns to greet his friends; a motley dozen in black.

'Ready?' he cheers.

Smoke floods the roof as the aster-lights swing.

A grinding warble reaches Jackson's ears: the hollow, howling whine that you hear in old films before the bombs start to fall. Arthur is still below but his outfit has loosened, his jacket open on a grubby vest. He cranks the rusty arm of an air-raid siren, old-style, howling in the night.

Caspar's group clink their bottles with each other, grinning. They light the rags on the flaming barrels and send them sailing down at Arthur's wall, a shower of amber. Bottles burst into flowers of flame. Soon other objects are burning. Low fire slithers and leaps through the heaped stuff of Arthur's wall. The wall was never meant to keep the blackvests out – not even Arthur was that crazed, that idealistic. He'd built the wall as a weapon, a trap that would catch fire, its gutter with petrol.

Someone calls his name. 'Jackson, I thought you left. Your brother—'

Lali sits with her back to the parapet. Her fingers skitter across the keyboard in her lap as tabs and windows multiply over her screen. One shows a feed of Marco's camera, a smear of fire-lit faces and shadowed plants. Others show streams, status updates, emails, and chat boxes, a shifting grid of interactions. She navigates the screen with a fluent haste, typing quickly, never blinking, a dawn-blue glow on her cheeks.

'This is so much bigger than us,' she says. 'Bigger than the Citadel, even.' She opens an email, subject heading: <3. The attachment shows a tower to the city's north, a banner hanging from the balcony, protestors gathered in the windows. 'We aren't alone,' says Lali. 'We started something.'

'We started throwing rocks,' says Jackson.

Lali tuts. 'Don't be so obtuse. That was Caspar, not me. Did you find him? Frank? He was up here just now. He was looking for you.'

'Where did he go? Where's Nell?'

'How should I know?'

Jackson is overcome by a weariness he can't explain, an inertia that pools in his stomach and weighs down his arms. He sits on the parapet's edge.

'We should have gone,' he says. 'We should have gone. We should have—'

'Gone? The whole point is to stay,' says Lali, 'even if we lose. Don't you get it? Being here – beaten, arrested even – all of it matters. It's doing something for once. Not just sitting there feeling depressed, or having arguments about—'

'I don't care about the Citadel,' says Jackson. 'I never did.'

'I know,' Lali replies. 'Precious Frank.'

'It wasn't about you either,' Jackson replies, 'if that's what you're thinking.' Lali's sheer cheeks and sharp nose are softened in the amber, but her eyes have that keen, snarling look he knows well. 'It was more than that. I was trying to work something out.'

'Jackson,' Lali gasps. 'This isn't a time for a fucking therapy session. We've talked already. I never made any promises. And now we're here on a fucking roof and it's fucking on fire and I'm fucking trying to fucking – wait... Where were you, anyway?' Lali asks. This whole time, she hasn't looked at him once. Her eyes have stayed fixed on the screen, that ferocious concentration he knows well. 'You just... went,' she says, 'right when we needed you.'

'I didn't think they'd come until dawn,' says Jackson. 'I thought—'

The truth is that he didn't think. It was a weekday. He went to work as planned. He painted walls with a break for lunch and his body was patterned a star-map of matt emulsion flecks. He finished at 7pm and he knew he should head straight back to the Citadel. His phone was in his pocket, but, consciously or otherwise, he hadn't charged it overnight; the screen was dead already. He pictured the crowds at the Citadel. He imagined the atmosphere: hope slowly crushed by the weight of an inevitable end. He would rather be anywhere else. Famished, he sat beneath a huge, shaggy tree in the park. The mood in the city shifted as daylight fell. Flotillas of cloud shed their misty payloads. When the park began to squall Jackson got on his bike and cycled through the rain to a busy square in which people were shopping, laughing, looking happy under neon, the flashing bright signs and enticements. He thought about the old office building he used to visit years ago with Frank, where, in anger at the District Institute, he would teach his brother lessons. In those days, in his mid-teens, his chest a barrel of feelings he could not name, his head a welter of indecisions and crass ideas that make him cringe, he leant on his younger brother more than Frank knew. He'd been cruel and controlling, he realised now, because he was frightened that Frank might leave him. He remembered that dark staircase and its old familiar smell, cringing at his self-directed sense of rebel heroism: how special he'd felt to have found it. People were drinking milkshakes, swinging bags of clothes. Elaborate fountains plashed. He wondered what the Citadel would look like a decade from now – he wondered if he cared, if the future was fixed or could be edited, written on a screen or on stone. He thought about Leonard: that tall and wild irascible moody creature who, despite being dead for years, still spoke clearly in Jackson's mind. He thought, to his surprise, about his mother, the dark ocean that swayed under stars, the emptiness that entered him, infected him, changed him, poisoned his DNA, that scorched afternoon in his childhood. When tiredness overcame him, he lay on his back in lateral glow of shopfronts until, without warning, he buckled. Sobs snapped through him like a series of electric shocks. His face was a mess of tears and snot. He made ugly barking noises like a donkey in distress. But beneath the spasms, beneath the anguish, he was confused, almost amused, by a question: why the fuck was he crying?

Frank crouches in the smouldering glow of the Citadel's yard. His ribs sting his chest as he inhales. The last few hours have been a treadmill. Corridors. Rooftops. Garden paths. He has been running for hours and his muscles burn. He has scanned every face and he has called out his brother's name. But no one is Jackson, his brother is lost.

Frank will run back to the boat. Fuck wishing that

Jackson will call, fuck trying to join a revolution he knew would fail, and fuck the risk. He will swallow his pride, like Leonard always said he should, and he will run back to the barge like a good boy, and wait.

Then he looks up.

A firework flares and in the light of its sputtering tracery he sees an outline of his brother. Perched on the parapet's edge with his head in his hands.

Frank cries out. He cannot help himself. His voice is a reedy whine against the discord of the night but he keeps on screaming his brother's name. Jackson. Jackson. But Jackson doesn't turn.

He can run back to the boat or he can run towards his brother.

If he stays, he will be caught; if he's caught he'll be arrested; if he's arrested he might as well die.

The blackvests have breached the front doors. Buckled plastic lies twisted and torn like surfboards washed up by a tidal wave. He slips past a lifter who reels in the wake of a blow – a protestor with bloodied teeth wields a plank of screw-studded wood.

Frank ducks past him and into the lobby – a blur of heat and a tussle of limbs. Grey boiler suits. Banners. White helmets. Chains. Bruised skin. Raised arms.

He dashes and ducks through the crowd like a fish through coral. A stray elbow smacks him in the cheek but he squirms loose and drops to all fours, forcing his way through a thicket of knees and shins. Phrases churn about his head like startled bats, a swirl of unfinished statements.

'You're a—'

'Fuck look what—'

'—puppet of—'

'—hurts it—'

'—will be—'
'—doing someone—'
'—on the—'
'—hurts it—'
'—stop him someone—'
'—back off, back – back – back—'
'—stop.'
He surfaces again in the kitchen corridor.
There.

Jackson stumbles down the stairwell, crashing against the wall. His eyes are empty and black as bullet holes. Ash is plastered to the sweat on his forehead. They run for the kitchen.

A young protestor, maybe fifteen years old, is in the middle of the room. He is armed with a wooden spoon and colander helmet, plastic bin lid as a shield. Over the toppled fridge, visible through the plastic-paned windows, red-orange sparks sputter and fly from the back door's frame. A grey blur of toothed metal slips through the lock and into the room. The door flies open.

There is nothing left to do but act like kids and hide.

A grey door off the kitchen opens onto a cramped room, roughly the size of a toilet cubicle, the crooked shelves laden with tins of ossified eggshell and bottles of bleach, a mop's head flopped in the corner like a lost toupee. Through the thin door the brothers hear the footsteps pounding through the kitchen, down the corridor, up the stairs. They wait in darkness, the strip of light under the door a flicker, black boots rushing past. Jackson leans against the door; the handle rattles but doesn't budge.

'*Your* fault,' he hisses a moment later. '*Idiot*. Coming back like that, for *what*?'

'I—'

136

'We're fucked. That's it.'

'I'm—'

'Gone. Over. *Done*.'

'Will you let me speak? If we're playing the blame game then I'm hardly the champion here. You fucked off. You went for—'

'*Shhhhh!*' he says, lashing out to kick his brother below the knee.

The corridor quietens. Bent double, Frank rubs his injured shin.

Jackson opens the door a sliver and peers through, squints, opens it wider, gestures at his brother to follow. Frank limps into the pale glare of striplights.

'Quiet,' Jackson hisses.

The corridor echoes with noises. Shouts, slammed doors, wolfish howls, the pop and tinkle of smashed glass, and a wheezy thumping like the beating of a huge, rust-riddled heart.

'We can't just leave them,' Frank hisses as they near the lobby.

'Yes we can,' Jackson hisses back. 'If we don't we're—'

'We can stop them,' says Frank, louder now. 'We just need *people*, that's what—'

'People don't matter,' Jackson shouts, grabbing his brother by the shoulders. 'None of this fucking *matters*, all of it's *bullshit*, we can't get out, we can't stop it, they've *won*, they *win*, it's what they fucking *do*, they crush us and they crush us until we're *dead*, we don't have *energy*, we give up, we give in, they beat us and they wrap our wrists in cable ties and push us face-first in the dirt, because of what? Because we made life hard for them, because we are *people*, and they fucking hate *people*, it isn't worth it, it isn't worth it, fucking *hell*, I can't, I can't, I can't.'

137

The words rush out in a torrent. Frank has never seen Jackson ramble like that, the hot gush of addled sentences, and he's too stunned to reply.

'Anyway,' Jackson says, tone switching so quickly it's like he never stumbled at all, 'I thought you wanted to leave? You were begging—'

'Not begging.'

'—us to – *grovelling* to leave. Have *anger*, Frank. If I die tomorrow—'

'Don't say that.'

'If I'm gone—'

'Don't say that.'

'If we don't get out of this, if I fall behind, if they catch me—'

'What?'

'Just run. Keep running. Promise.'

'Where?'

'It doesn't matter. I'll find you.'

The lobby is almost deserted. A row of handcuffed protesters kneel as if awaiting a firing squad: wrists tied behind their backs, heads lowered, faces bloody and slicked with spit. A trio of blackvests stands watch. And there's the lifter Jackson tussled with earlier, out near the gate, the one who kicked him in the ribs. He's missing his helmet, his boiler suit slathered with mud. He turns and shouts as the brothers pace over the broken doors and into the rush of the rain-whipped air.

Arthur's wall is ruined. The flames have died to smoking shards and twisted husks. The windows of the glass towers over the plywood are broken, glass panes jagged, yawning. The Citadel's roof blazes like the head of a match, an angry knot of flames.

A trio of protestors have chained themselves to barrels in a corner of the roof; a blackvest ascends on a cherry picker. A protestor fumbles a purple flare and slips on the parapet's rain-slicked edge. She hangs from the roof by her fingers, by the chains wrapped tight round her chest: the others grab her shirt and tug upwards but she's slipping, slipping, caught in an awkward harness of fabric and chains.

The brothers see all this as a slow-motion blur, a rush of light glanced in the slip of their vision.

Frank lags. The lifter is behind them already, keeping pace as the brothers run.

The Citadel's grounds enclose them, slippery and labyrinthine, twisted paths unravelling as they run until, abruptly, they hit the open space of the driveway.

Blackvests throng the gate. Arrested protestors are being guided into open vans. Wrists cable-tied, they sulk and spit. A beam swings over Jackson, a bleaching flash. For an instant he feels like an angel, a luminous thing, his scrawny arms ablaze with white fire.

When the light fades he knows he's alone. His brother is lost somewhere behind him, lost in the thickets of weeds.

He sees the smashed windows and dancing bodies on the roof of the glass towers, the aster's swinging beam, thick plumes of purple smoke, and, rushing towards him down the path, a lifter. His dull grey boiler suit a perfect camouflage against the shadows. Jackson grips the brick and sets it loose. He turns to run before it lands but hears the thud and the howl behind him.

Cars stream over the flyover. The bright lights of the shopping mall leak into the sky and taint it red, white, violet. Water glitters in a gap between buildings, a black flatness fizzy with rain. Under the skittering beat of his heart he hears the glassy hush of it flooding, rich in rain, ready to carry him out of the city.

He reaches the wall in a handful of strides and sees the canal through the slit in the panels. The toothed edge of the plywood nips the hem of his coat as he edges through and snaps shut behind him.

A lifter's boot crunches on concrete: Jackson turns. The man's boiler suit is sodden, dark with dirt. For a second they watch each other, immobile, two figures in the slanting dark. Asters shudder. Sirens howl.

Jackson runs to the barge in a handful of strides but the lifter is quicker, stronger. He slips on the rain-glossed deck, catching a glimpse of the flag as he falls, a ragged streak of fabric in the rain. The lifter knees Jackson in the small of his spine and bends his mouth to Jackson's ear.

'It hurts more if you fight it.'

He can taste the lifter's uniform. Its fabric has absorbed the harshness of smoke, the trapped-animal stink of sweat. The lifter is heavy but quick. He mushes Jackson's nose against the rasping deck. Dirt on his teeth. Rain in his throat. The lifter shifts his tone, becomes imploring, matey: not an adversary but a friend.

'Listen mate, it's nothing. I tie you up, you come with me, and then it's over. Simple. Quick. I'm only doing my job.'

Jackson's head has been yelling like a fire alarm, a panic so total and shrill all sound is subsumed into its piercing trill. Now the energy left in him drains from his arms. He stops writhing for air, like a landed fish. He'll give up, give in. Surrender feels blissful and bleak in equal measure. The pressure of decisions and the itching of anger melt to liquid, fade: he is a vessel of resignation and numb fatigue. His body grows still, his eyes unfocused. The lifter tugs a cable tie from his pocket, knees crushing the muscles at Jackson's spine. In one

140

practised, careless gesture, he grabs Jackson's wrists and yanks them tight with a quick zipping sound.

'There,' the man says, squatting. 'Done.' He pauses. Something in his silence feels considered, hesitant, as though he is balancing his words before he speaks again.

The flyover's bright lights seem to fade, and at the edges of that darkness another figure appears, a slender silhouette, arm raised. Hood up, he swallows the gap between boat and wall in a fluent leap that makes no sound. The heavy thing hangs in his hand. Its curled tongs and its blunt head catch the light.

Figures are frozen in brief tableaux. In the foreground: the lifter's muscled shoulders and stubbled skull. Behind him: the frail figure of the hammer-wielding boy.

Jackson stares into the blank of his brother's open hood. He wants to cry out and tell him to run, but then he doesn't need to: Frank lowers the hammer slowly, halfway to disarming himself, when the lifter jerks upright, opens his mouth.

'I—'

Frank swings the hammer – the man's head whips to one side. The sound is sudden and unnaturally loud, a thunderclap crunching of bone. Sprawled on the boat's roof, skull slick with blood, the lifter stares dumb at the sky. Frank lifts the hammer and strikes again. The lifter's body snaps limp.

Jackson kneels on the boat, hands tied behind him, and looks up at his younger brother. Frank lit from behind by fire. He holds the hammer in his hand, the blunt tip dripping with blood.

V. FIRST LIGHT

The man lies flat on the sand, legs outstretched, arms at rest. His eyes are closed but his mouth is open, slack lips parted on the dark red muscle of his tongue. In the sockets of his eyes, the flesh is patterned with shades of lavender, ash, and sulphur, the soft meat swollen and deeply bruised. Weeds, sprouting from a slope of shingle, form a crooked halo around his head. Their bony trunks pierce a tangle of rust-coloured seaweed, which is shrivelled-up, jewelled with salt. Jackson inspects the plants. The brittle canes are hung with rattling seed-pods, spiked with thorny leaves and needles pale as bone. Harsh gusts quicken the churning waves. The dry weeds shiver.

Jackson turns to his younger brother, who is standing a short way further down the beach.

'Is he really dead?' Frank asks. His voice is thin, distant.

'I don't know,' Jackson replies. 'Is he breathing?'

'Doesn't look like he's breathing.'

'We need a mirror.'

Dawn is breaking on the estuary, wads of cloud soaked in colourless light. Hair worms over Frank's forehead, reaching into his eyes. He squints askance at Jackson.

'A mirror?'

'You're meant to hold one up to his mouth,' says Jackson. 'See if you get condensation. That's how you know for sure.'

He clutches himself, a reflex. He is cold to his marrow.

'Says who?'

Jackson shrugs. 'Can't remember.'

The shoreline is wind-scoured, blasted, bleak. Old battlements hunker down the sand, obsolete defences that resemble totems now, crumbled by age and weather.

Their innards are riddled with nets of wire and mottled with luminous algae.

Frank runs a hand through his wet black hair. Raindrops leap and seethe as they hit the sand.

'We don't have a mirror,' says Frank. He folds his arms, copying Jackson, to preserve what little warmth is left in his shivering body. 'We don't *need* a mirror.' He recoils a few inches, snarling. 'Look at him,' he says. '*Look.*'

Jackson would rather not.

'Alright,' he says.

The sand is chicken-poxed with blotches of oil. Heaps of knotted seaweed straggle the sand in clumps. Further up, beyond the chattering weeds, is a bank of rubbish. Dumped, a rusting, gutted washing machine, crushed beer cans glinting, a headless action figure, needle-thin fish spines, a stray flip-flop, tangled nets, and punctured buoys. Maybe they should leave the man here, Jackson wonders. An offering to the ocean, its hunger for tidal trash.

'Check his pulse,' he says.

'No,' Frank snaps. 'You do it.'

'It's easy. Just your thumb against his neck, here,' he says, showing Frank the spot on his own neck, 'and see if you can feel the pulse.'

A silence swells between them. Side by side, they stare at the man. It is hard to tell how old he is. His thinning hair forms a widow's peak, is shot through with grey at the temples. His forehead is deeply lined: the creases look carved by a knife. But there's a youthful plumpness in the swell of his wide, unwrinkled cheeks, his parted lips. He could be sleeping in a cot.

'I'm not touching him,' says Frank. 'Let's just go. Leave him. Cover him up with—'

'We can't just *leave him*,' Jackson cuts in.

'—rocks and. What?'

'We can't leave him,' Jackson says, louder.

'*Bury* him, not just *leave* him.'

'If he's alive, if he wakes up—'

'Dead guys don't wake up,' Frank yells.

'But if he *does*—'

'You wanna call the police?'

Drops of rain flick from Jackson's nose, chin, ears as he shakes his head. His raincoat hangs open, limp as a rag, the damp and airless plastic sucking at the skin of his arms. The man is missing one shoe, his left.

'What, then?' Frank asks. 'We don't have all day, do we? He's d—' He stops. His mouth hangs open, eyes unfocused. 'Dead,' he says. The word is barely audible above the cackle of faraway gulls.

'I don't know what to do,' Jackson admits. 'Don't know anything any more.'

Strange colours churn in the brightening sky: seaweed-green, mussel-shell blue, shot through with fissures of grey. He has been avoiding his reflection for most of his life, but earlier, washing his hands in the boat's cramped bathroom, he caught a glimpse of himself in the window. The high, gaunt cheekbones. The pale lips. The buzzed hair crazily uneven. And that look in those eyes, *his* eyes, like a stranger staring back.

'He's dead,' says Frank.

He picks up a long blond branch and prods the man's belly, exposed by a gash in his clothing, the heavy flesh thatched with black hairs. The skin puckers. The man doesn't flinch or groan. When Frank lifts the stick again, the puckered star stays white. He looks at Jackson. A slick of blood reddens his cheek like lipstick gone awry.

'Try again,' says Jackson. 'Harder. In the neck.'

'He's *dead*, Jackson. *Dead*.'

146

'Could be concussed.'

'Look at him. Look at his lips. Have you ever seen lips that colour? Does he *look* concussed?'

'A coma, then.'

'Are you *mental*? We dropped him twice – and nothing, nothing, he's gone.'

Arkady is beached in the shallows. Lopsided in the tide, its black underside faces the shore. Looking at it now, Jackson marvels that the boat made it this far. Its sides, in a previous life, were ink-black and cherry-red, but the colours have since degraded, with scabrous imperfections where the paint has flaked away to reveal the dull metal beneath. The driver's cabin is patched together with lengths of scrap, nails and screws jutting crookedly from the corners.

'*Think*,' says Jackson. He hasn't slept properly in days. He smacks himself in the forehead, punches himself in the thigh. Pain brings him back to his senses. Everything is the colour it should be, but starker, more luminous.

'We should bury him,' says Frank.

'With what? Where?'

'Here,' says Frank, kneeling down, 'on the beach, with our hands.'

The flatness of the marshes is unbroken by mountain or town. Tangled waterways and acres of reeking, sliding mud are interrupted only by boxy factories, steaming power plants, and the swooping wires of the skeletal pylons that march inland. Jackson feels, in the midst of this openness, dangerously exposed. The land is squashed flat by the weight of the sky and the sea goes on forever.

He stares inland, yearning for a warm, dry room.

'I'll do it,' says Frank.

Frank is at Jackson's ankles now. He scrabbles at the

beach with both hands. He's still wearing the hoodie Jackson stole for him months ago, his favourite. Black, it has a white 7 on the breast pocket: Frank's lucky number. The sand grows darker the deeper he goes. His fingernails dig up coal-black sand, white chunks of plastic, dead crustaceans' severed legs.

'We have to put him back on the boat,' says Jackson. 'Sail out over the water there, miles out. Bury him at sea.'

He realised it just now, watching his brother dig.

'But it's working,' says Frank. 'Look.' He points at the hole he has made. Water weeps off the sides and gathers at the bottom. 'We can do it with our hands,' says Frank. The water's surface dimly shimmers with reflected sky.

'I know we can,' Jackson snaps. 'That's not the issue.'

'We can do it, here – trust me, it'll work.'

Looking down at his brother, Jackson catches sight of his own chest through the gap in his raincoat. The fabric of his T-shirt is crusted with mud and engine-oil. Another shade is mixed up among the blackish brown: a congealed stain leaking crimson tendrils as the rain flows down the fabric. Instinctively he zips the raincoat closed, hiding the blood from view.

'No,' says Frank, shaking his head. 'Look at this place. No one will find him. Let's do it now. Quick.'

Jackson's mind goes blank. He twists his neck to glance upriver, where a ship just sounded its foghorn, filling the sky with noise. A chunk is missing from his memory. The man was upright, then he wasn't; he was standing, then flat on the boat. Alive. Then half-alive. And now, it seems, dead.

Last night, after they left the Citadel, the barge swung heavily into the darkness and down the waters of the canal. The Citadel was burning behind them, its roof alive with fire, black smoke rising in a vertical column into the blurred amber sky. Fumes of burning plastic swam through the wind. Shadows stretched and shifted as the asters' searchlights swung, searching out protestors who'd fled.

How many had been arrested by then?

As *Arkady* floated down kinked canals and through the city's amber grid, Jackson felt certain they'd be caught. Their boat would turn white as the searchlights' beams converged. A policeman on the creek's bank would spot them sliding past and jump aboard.

But neither of those things happened – and soon the brothers reached the river. The water's surface was patterned with sinuous currents that reflected the glare of the flames. They were out in the open, aimless, drifting with the flow.

Frank was calm. Too calm. He stood on the boat's deck, wind in his hair, watching the lights of the riverbank as if they belonged to a fairground. Jackson steered where his instincts pulled him: away from the city, towards the darkness of the widening estuary.

'You know what this means,' says Jackson, coming back to his senses. He reminds himself to be practical, focus on tasks, not get sunk into quagmires of memory.

Frank smears his fingers on his jeans to clean them. He opens his mouth but says nothing.

'We're never coming back,' says Jackson. 'Never. Understand? From now on we're different people. Different names. They'll be looking for us already – they'll have our names, photos. Keep going. Never stop.'

Frank nods. 'I thought that was always the plan.'

'It was a stupid plan,' says Jackson, filled with spite at his former self, the one who believed the plan might work. Drifting where the waters guided them, unwatched, directionless, free, he and Frank would live, for once, on their own terms, together and free. It was as simple and as naïve as that: a bid for freedom, independence, and a fuck-you to a city that scorned them.

When did the idea begin, exactly? When he saw the boat, or sooner?

He has been planning this journey for years – maybe decades, if you count the first time he felt that yearning to get out, lying in his bed in the bedsit, staring at the wall – and this is where it ends: a dead beach at the end of the world.

Jackson bends at the waist, strange lights pulsing in his eyes.

'The plan was good,' says Frank. 'It just went... wonky, that's all.'

A gust thumps off the crashing waves. The weeds' canes hiss.

They shovel handfuls of clammy, compacted sand, digging like dogs. Jackson pulls his hood up, shielding his face from the rain: a damp cave of sound. Wind flows over the marshes, scouring the shore. The mad gulls scream as they wheel overhead.

Digging rhythmically, automatically, he is overcome, for the second time since they came ashore, by the feeling of dislocation or floating. His mind, slipping loose of his skull, haunts the air behind him like a ghost. This is not his body any more. He is watching a film about something that happened, or might have happened, to someone else, years ago, on a different continent, a made-up world. The feeling surges, fades, surges again, rhythmic as the waves that lurch and suck behind him.

A tarmac path traces the curve of the shore. It runs along the outer wall of a factory: a sprawl of low buildings assembled from metal sheets and breezeblocks, and crowned with silver tubes. The tubes leak thick white clouds that stretch into giant eels before deforming and dissolving, faded and vague in the rain. Red lights burn at the towers' tips but he can see no signs of life.

He looks at the hole they have dug: a foot deep at its deepest point, steadily filling with water.

'It's not working,' he says.

'It is,' says Frank, his fingers claggy with sand, 'it's working fine. Look,' he says, digging faster, '*look*.'

'I'm looking.'

The path stretches off past a clump of thorny bushes. Near the jetty it veers sharply inland, the turning marked by a rusted post. Dull heat pushes at the rear of his skull.

'Stop,' he says.

'Why?' Frank replies, irritated. 'We've only just—'

'Look,' he says, pointing. 'There – past the bushes.'

He hadn't seen them before. Their shell-pale colours camouflaged them in the marshes, their crouching, flat-roofed structures merging with the scrub. But there is no mistaking the brick-like shape of them. People live here, within a few hundred feet of the body. A red towel swings on a clothesline strung between two bungalows.

'We can't, not here,' he says, crouching. 'Look – some-one will see him. A dog-walker, anyone – they'll find the body and run the tests and—'

'I'm not touching him again,' says Frank.

'We have to. Haven't you ever watched TV?'

'What's this got to do with—'

'Tests. DNA, fingerprints. One of those white tents – we're all over this place. We might as well hand our-selves in. You want that?'

'We could...' Frank pauses, thinks. 'We could wait until someone else came along. Explain what happened

– tell the truth.'

Jackson shakes his head.

'Why not?' says Frank.

'Who would believe us?'

Jackson slips his hands under the man's armpits and round, hooking the shoulders. The skull rests against his chest, slack cheeks shaking with every step. Frank waddles backwards, lurching with the weight. How long since he slept, since he ate?

The tide is higher than it was before, lapping at their knees. Jackson's clothes are soaked already. He hardly feels the cold.

Frank loosens his grip when they near the boat. The man's legs lollop into the water. Without a word, Frank clambers up the boat's angled side: a swift, smooth leap, tugging buoys and railings as he climbs.

Even now, even here, there is wonder in the world. Jackson marvels at his brother's swiftness, the liquid grace with which he moves.

Frank steps into the wheelhouse, leaving Jackson alone with the body. He drags it to a bank of dry sand and lays it down.

From this angle, he cannot see the wound itself, just the dark and reddish blurs of blood that stain the skull.

Staring at his face, its waxy cast, Jackson feels almost sorry for the man. He wants to wash the blood from his skull, clean the sand from his skin, heal the leaking wound, fix him. The man's eyes are closed now. But earlier, in the darkness, in the rain, he saw them staring into his. Gently, he places his boot on the lifter's throat. He pushes lightly; then harder, harder still. The oesophagus yields beneath his weight, like a rubber tube. The muscles tighten.

'What you doing?'

Frank is on the boat's roof, a length of thick nylon rope wrapped round his shoulder, a puzzled look on his face.

'Nothing,' says Jackson, lifting his boot. 'Get down here.'

They set about tying the body, looping the rope around the feet and the legs to bind them, folding the arms across the man's chest and binding the torso too, threading the rope from ankle to shoulder, under and through the loops, knotting the ends and pulling them tight, leaving two lengths trailing at feet and head. They grab a loop at either end, squat down, and straighten their spines.

'Ready?' says Jackson.

Frank nods. They lift.

'Will it hold?' Frank asks.

'Has to,' Jackson replies.

Frank leaps up the boat's side once again. Jackson chucks up one of the lengths; Frank grabs it, ties it to the railing; and they repeat the process for the feet. The body hangs against the boat's side, bent at the waist – a buoy.

'I need a hand,' says Jackson. Frank leans over to help him up, and he is surprised by how easily he climbs. He feels almost weightless, scooped hollow, his bones as light as balsa wood. On the boat, Jackson pauses, leans forward, and breathes. Tiny fireworks dance across his eyes.

'You alright?' says Frank.

'Just need a second.'

'You're fine. You're fine. Right?'

He watches the estuary, its dancing light. A raincloud like a tectonic plate imposes itself on the distance.

'Shut up,' he says.

Boats have appeared upriver: ferries and cruisers, chunky tugs and hulking ships criss-crossing the water's breadth. The river will only get worse, grow more crowded, as the morning progresses.

'Alright,' says Jackson. 'Let's go.'

They loop the rain-soaked rope around their forearms, feet squashed hard against the edge of the boat, leaning back with all their weight. Inch by inch, hand by hand, they lift the body. Frank lets the rope slip a couple of times and stands breathless, groaning, staring at his bleeding palms. Soon the man is high enough for Jackson to lean across and grip the loops. The body wobbles, slips, and slips again, never quite leaning far enough to clear the rim. Muscles burning, tendons stretch at ankle and neck.

The body dumps onto the roof with a reverberant clang.

'Fuck-fuck-fuck-fuck,' Frank hisses, blowing on his rope-burnt hands.

Jackson slides to his knees, sucking ragged gulps of air. The man's head is turned away, face in the gutter. His scalp is capped with matted hair and blood.

'Can it stop now?' Jackson says, staring at a patch of rust.

'What?' Frank gasps; he spits into the sea. 'I think I'm about to—'

Hands on thighs, knees on metal, Jackson thumps his head against the wheelhouse. Frank is at the front. Gripping the railing, he retches overboard.

'You okay?' Jackson asks a moment later.

Frank turns to face his brother, bloodless face tinged green.

'You mean apart from the fact we just lifted a *dead* guy onto a boat and it almost killed me and then I was sick?'

he shouts. 'Oh yeah. I'm fine, totally fine. Thrilled. Ecstatic. Thanks.'

They haul the body to the bedroom at the back of the boat and lay the man onto the floor. His head leans at an awkward angle. His hands are folded in his lap like nesting birds. His legs are straight, the shoeless foot swollen by seawater. The blue ropes, loosened now around his shoulders and legs, cradle him like a fishing net.

'Wait...' says Frank.

'What?'

Jackson looks at Frank; Frank looks at the man. 'I just...' A dark thought swims across the edge of his awareness, like an eel sliding through shadowy weeds; a moment later, it is gone.

'What?' Jackson barks.

'Something's not right.'

'You just noticed?'

Jackson watches the beach through the rain-dappled windows. White churn edges the breakers. The tide is rising, washing the brothers' footprints away and sucking the boat's black sides. Purple has faded to pink: light distils itself through clouds. It gleams on the metal dashboard, the cracked varnish of the wooden wheel. An aura warms the edges of the gearstick.

'Get outside,' says Jackson. 'Boat might be stuck.'

He twists the key. The engine rumbles in the bowels of the boat. Slowly, the barge throbs to life. Vibrations rise through the floor into the bones of Jackson's feet, shins, thighs, and spine. When he hears it in his skull – that barely audible hum in the bones of his ears – he knows the engine is ready.

The gears grumble. Something's wrong.

Jackson feels it in the pinioned rocking of the boat, the engine thrashing in the shallows: the barge's nose is lodged in the sand. He had been in such a panic, the boat lumbering headlong through choppy surf, his head so crammed with thoughts, asters in the sky, black-vests with truncheons and tasers, cramped cold cells in unlisted facilities, that he forgot to kill the engine. The boat thumped headfirst into the beach. Pans and plates and glasses tumbled crashing to the floor. Jackson slammed into the wheel, which smacked the air from his lungs.

'It's not moving,' Frank yells again, louder.

'Push it.'

'I am, it's not—'

'Just *push* it,' Jackson screams.

Frantic, he tugs the lever back and forth to rev the engine. The boat lurches and churns, creaking as it tugs against its socket of molten sand. Frank yells out – then Jackson feels it. A lingering, sliding movement, a sudden wrench.

The barge is floating.

He rolls the wheel to the right. The room floods with petrol fumes and the iodine smell of the water. Frank flops over the railing, soaked.

'You were leaving without me,' he pants, slouching into the wheelhouse doorway.

Land falls away in the windows. Details blur and merge. Soon the beach is a dark line trimmed with greenery. He turns the wheel, swings the boat around until it faces the bright horizon, and shifts the gearstick forward.

Arkady floats without shelter or camouflage, as exposed as an ant on a page. Jackson tilts his head, drums his fingers on the wheel. He follows the darting arcs of gulls.

'There,' he says, pointing. 'They're looking for us.'

Shipping containers. Silt mines. Nothing.

'Who?' says Frank.

Only a trace of the strangeness of dawn remains: a ripple of lavender, skirted with rose, hangs banner-like over the northern shore.

'That thing?' he asks.

Jackson jabs again, once, at the window.

All Frank can see is the land.

The marshes here are overgrown with tentacles of industry, tubes, pipes, tunnels, and wires that infiltrate the tidal territories. Factories mine the salt-stiffened earth for minerals, fuel to feed the server farms. Smokestacks leak vapours into the breeze. Chemicals flaring to life as they react with the open air.

'There,' says Jackson, 'right there – *look*.'

It flashes: a circular blur. Another. A swarm of fly-black asters high above the city.

'They've seen us,' says Jackson, 'followed us to the boat and – you said there weren't any cameras—'

'There weren't.'

'—and that no one saw you and—'

'They didn't.'

'—you said, you *said*—'

'There's no way anyone saw us,' says Frank.

The canal was empty. Darkness shot through with slivers of rain, the buildings blank. The brothers were alone with the lifter.

'Explain *that*, then,' Jackson says.

The asters strafe across the northeast edge of the motorway. The city's buried rivers resurface there, un-spooling through outer suburbs.

Settlements have grown across treacherous land. Droves of people have left the city centre and built improvised villages. Tents, huts, mossy caravans have begun to spring up there, on the sliding earth.

'Someone must have seen us,' says Jackson, 'one of the others told the police, gave them a description – they'll have dozens of them—'

'It's not for us,' says Frank. 'Why would they bother with us?'

'Are you kidding? They think we killed someone,' says Jackson. 'One of their own.'

The asters lift and veer. They fly southwest in a smooth and windblown curve. Paused again on the sky-line, they hang like a chandelier.

'We *did* kill someone though,' says Frank.

'Well yeah, I know that, I just mean... We can't do it,' says Jackson, watching the asters shrink to black specks. 'Not here. Anyone could see us.'

'There's no one for miles,' says Frank.

'I don't mean the water, idiot. The skies.'

The skies, if anything, are even emptier. There is only the shrouded sun, its muffled light; the asters in the middle distance, far enough away the brothers can't hear their wings; and the planes rising and falling, as though on conveyor belts of air, into and out of the offshore airport.

'Where, then?' says Frank.

'Somewhere else.'

'There is nowhere else.'

Frank scans the northern shore. Floating cities have docked at port. Cranes and robot arms are busy scanning, winching, lifting, and unloading the bright containers off the hulking ships. The port runs like a wind-up toy. No living creatures in sight. But the shore is watched by cameras, patrolled by guards.

Tidal islands dot the waters beyond the port. Dull grey, they merge with the waves that bathe them.

Frank remembers the map. The blank patch, the dotted red line. Months ago, when they were refurbishing the boat, he researched the canal network, the ports, and the estuary, scoping out places to moor.

'We'll drop him there,' says Frank, 'out by that orange buoy. If he washes up, no one will find him.'

'How do you know? It's the city. Everywhere's bad.'

The army owns the silvery spits of land. They use it for testing weapons. Bombs and bullets are absorbed and erased by the liquid mud. Sometimes the explosions can be felt from the city, bass-thumps resonating in the cavity of your chest. From here it looks like nothing, just an empty stretch of land.

'Government owns it,' says Frank. 'No one lives there.'

Jackson tilts his head at the window. His cropped hair glows.

'Alright,' he sighs, frowning. His head hangs loose. 'There's nowhere else to go.'

'Don't be like that,' says Frank.

'Like what?'

'Moaning. Sighing. Giving up.'

'How the fuck am I meant to act?'

'I don't know, I'm just saying. It could be worse.'

'*Could be worse*?'

The wheelhouse door is open. A cold, clean smell of salt flows in.

'It could always be worse,' says Frank. 'You could be dead. I could be dead.'

Jackson scans the horizon. Another plane rises; another plane lands.

'Kind of wish I was dead,' he says.

'But you're not.'

'Guess so.'

'And it had to be one of us, didn't it?'

Jackson grips the wheel. The clouds have begun to break open, thaw. Light like meltwater drenches the port.

'So it had to be him.'

'I know,' says Jackson. 'I'm just... tired. My brain. It's stopped working. I try and think about things and nothing, my head fogs up. I feel like I'm not inside myself. Does that make sense?'

Frank shrugs.

'We got any whiskey left?' Jackson asks, brightness flaring in his eyes.

'Maybe,' says Frank. The brothers keep alcohol under the sink, cheap spirits and cans of beer. But with the last few weeks at the Citadel, the long drunken night by the bonfire, slugging murky cocktails for added warmth, Frank suspects it's all used up. 'I'll check,' he says.

The tide is strong in this part of the estuary. It coaxes *Arkady* towards the shore. Through the slits in the curtains Frank picks out leafless trees, their twisted forms confused with nearby pylons and the skeletal cranes of the port. Further off is the city. Distance has compressed the jutting towers, skinny skyscrapers, office blocks, and looping overpasses into a low haze. Sunlight flashes off windows and curtain walls. The city glimmers like a spillage of quartz.

Something rattles to Frank's right as he walks: insect-clicks of cutlery as forks and spoons rock back and forth on ceramic tile.

The floor is littered with broken glass. To his immediate right is the kitchen, grubby gaps where the fridge and the hob would stand. Toppled tins of food and heaps of crockery crowd the cupboards. Plates lie shattered on the floor in sharp white chunks, like sharks' teeth.

160

Frank's body has stiffened against the sight of the man, who haunts the corner of the room. He glances over, unable to help himself.

Swaddled in his boiler suit, wrapped in a truss of blue rope, the man is. His face is hidden beneath a tea towel and his legs are stretched.

'Whiskey,' Frank says to no one, distracting himself from the body, reminding himself of his task.

He opens the cupboard under the sink. Cleaning products. Tools.

Maybe his brother was right. Frank feels outside himself, behind himself, watching his hands through a telescope's lens.

Lurking at the back beneath a crisp blue husk of an ancient J-cloth is a vodka bottle, roughly a quarter full. Frank unscrews the cap and sniffs. He drinks a slug.

The burn in his throat fades to numbness; the numbness brings relief.

'Got some,' he shouts.

He feels instantaneously drunk. The room takes on an edge of giddy delirium, atoms throbbing in the gloom.

No reply. The engine must have muffled his voice.

'Jackson?'

Nothing.

He shrugs, tucks the bottle into his jacket pocket.

Instead of walking towards the wheelhouse door, his legs carry him into the boat.

Through swaying curtains to his right he sees nothing but ocean. Low, muted sounds move through the boat, the thock and slump of waves as they trouble the hull.

Vodka sloshes in Frank's pocket as he walks. There is music in his head, a haunting, looping melody that always features in his dreams about drowning. A shoal of notes hang in the air.

The coffee table comes into view. Its surface is a chaos of papers, books, itineraries, articles. The brothers' plans – drawn, refined, erased, and re-drawn with a meticulous self-importance – embarrass Frank. He wants to burn them, forget them.

The boat abruptly lurches as Jackson turns the wheel. Frank reaches out to steady himself on a window. His hand leaves a print of condensation on the pane. Splayed fingers. It looks like a starfish.

He takes another slug of vodka. Fortified, he looks down.

Maybe it's just the weather. Maybe it's just the light. But something about the man has changed, an almost imperceptible shift.

Frank leans forward, panic overpowering restraint. He plucks the tea towel off the man's head. His stare darts up and down.

The foot looks the same, swollen and pale. The legs are tied together, as before. The head is tilted towards the stove, the temple resting against the black metal, the hairline flush with the handle's edge. The mouth hangs slightly open. Nothing has moved or altered. If it has, the boat's motion explains it – its cradle-like, back-and-forth rocking.

When the brothers carried the body through earlier, and laid it out on the floor, pausing briefly to catch their breath and look into each other's eyes, the man's palms were loosely clasped. The palms faced each other, as if in prayer, the knuckles' bony ridges exposed.

Now the hands are open. The inner wrists are visible, their branching veins vivid blue. A tiny scar, shaped like a comma, brightens the skin of a finger.

Frank examines the head again. He follows the line

of the stubbled jaw to the earlobe, along the cheekbone, to the eyeballs nestled in their caves of bruised skin. From the eyelids, Frank examines the nose, the cartilage slightly bent where the head's weight presses it into the metal.

His gaze trails the short distance from the base of the nose to the mouth. The lips are parted, as before, although their colour is different: less blue.

The teeth are visible, as before.

Here is the difference, finally, so small he could have easily missed it: on the ruby-dark lower lip, a bubble forms.

Collapses.

Forms again.

Frank slams through the open door and crashes shoulder-first into the control panel. He stares at Jackson with flung-wide, blinkless eyes.

'Why—' Jackson begins to ask, but the look on his brother's face stops him.

'You need to see – to see,' Frank blurts.

'See what?'

'The guy – the man,' he gasps, 'the body – the person we – back in the – fuck – I mean – Jackson he—'

'What—'

'—killed but he – you have to – we—'

'Frank, slow down.'

'—I just walked in – and – he was – he was – I think he was—'

'Have you been drinking?'

'A bubble.'

'What?'

'A bubble – on his lip.'

'A *bubble*,' says Jackson.

'I think – the man – he's...'

'There's vodka in your pocket.'

'He's *breathing*.'

'He isn't breathing.'

'He is!' Frank snaps. 'You didn't see him – I saw him – I saw—'

'Dead people don't breathe,' says Jackson. 'How much is left? You didn't finish it, did you?'

'I'm serious – stood there and—'

'Bubbles, *yes*. You said,' says Jackson. 'A bubble. Pass the bottle. I can't believe you just tucked in without me.'

'Listen to me!'

Jackson swigs and winces. Tears brighten his eyes. He inhales once, very slowly. Eyes closed, he shakes his head. 'Better,' he says.

'His *lips* though,' says Frank. 'It was on his lips. It came out, and then—'

'He's wet,' says Jackson. He swallows another mouthful, dries his mouth with the back of his hand, and plonks the bottle on the control panel: a dulled clunk of glass on wood. *Arkady* has strayed a long way down the shore, but the orange buoy still looks far away. 'Wet things make bubbles,' says Jackson. 'It was nothing.'

Frank curls his toes in his sodden boots. His hands ball themselves into impotent fists. 'You're being an irresponsible adult,' he snaps.

The words surprise both of the brothers.

'Wow,' says Jackson. A grin spreads over his face. 'Alright then, kid. What do you want?'

The light that fills the cabin is tinted and textured by water, filtered by rainclouds and mirrored by sea. Daylight dissolves through the curtains, reaching towards, but not quite touching, the shadowed far reach of the room. Dust-motes sway like plankton. They drift open in spiralling shoals as Jackson kneels.

'Look,' says Frank. *'There.'*

'I can't see a bubble.'

'It was there, right there,' says Frank, jabbing.

'You sure?'

'I saw it. *I saw it.* Just wait.'

Jackson, squatting, does not wait. Instead, he lifts the man's wrist. The motion is delicate, slow, as though the man's body was spun from glass. Jackson peels the boiler suit back to the elbow, clearing the skin, then pushes his thumb into the man's wrist, his eyes on the man's shrouded face. Skin creases where Jackson presses into it, pressure firm as he digs for a pulse.

'Can you feel anything?' Frank asks. He tightens his grip on the hammer. It is more of a talisman now than a weapon or tool. Proof that he has mastered the man already: proof that he can do it again.

'Be quiet,' Jackson says.

Frank's shoulders drop. The procedure unfolds.

The measured pace with which Jackson works reminds Frank of the times he was sick or injured himself, lying on a mattress, crying at the pain of cracked ribs, bruised muscles, bleeding wounds. Jackson would nourish Frank's cuts with antiseptic, seal the deepest gashes with needle and thread. He poured numbing slugs of vodka into Frank's mouth, fed him pills. It was an extension of everything else. Jackson as brother, parent, instructor, friend, protector, rival, nurse.

Jackson lowers the man's arm so it lies at his side, palm-down on the carpet. He glances at Frank. His eyes are dark.

'I knew it,' says Frank.

They don't have an anchor. They can't let *Arkady* drift into open waters, or crash onto government land. And so they moor the boat to the first solid thing they can find.

Frank stands out front whilst Jackson steers. The engine shudders. Smoke purls in the breeze. Frank flings a loop of rope around the wood and ties it firm. Jackson kills the engine. *Arkady* tugs the stump like a dog on a leash.

'Where the fuck are we now?' says Jackson.

'I don't know,' says Frank. He racks his brain, scanning his memorised map. 'Birds,' he says.

'Birds?'

'Yeah,' says Frank. 'And power stations. Trees.'

'I said *where are we*, not *let's play a fucking game of I Spy*.'

Beyond the stump is a pebbled beach; beyond that a low wall, a signposted path running past it. Fresh tarmac. Further still are the sculpted reed-beds and zig-zagging paths of the nature reserve. Birds move darkly in sinuous skeins. Others hang lonely in higher air, resting their wings on the wind.

'We're here,' says Frank. 'We're somewhere. Who cares what it's called.'

Jackson grips the railing, scans the path. 'It looks like a place. A proper place. Money. People nearby. Not like before.'

'Before was different,' says Frank.

'How?'

'He was dead.'

Frank parts the curtains of two sea-facing windows. It's a risk but the brothers need light. They lay the man out on the carpet. The ropes have begun to unravel, yet they cradle him, still, in a net of restriction. If he wakes and attempts to attack them, he will wriggle and squirm like a fish.

'*There*,' says Frank.

He splashes water across the man's face. The man does not flinch. Water pools in his eye sockets, his ear.

'Twice now,' says Jackson. 'Nothing.'

166

'I told you,' said Frank. 'The sea would have done it. Water won't work.'

Jackson, frowning, places the tips of his index and middle fingers over his mouth, just beneath his nose. He does this whenever he's deep in thought.

'How hard did you hit him?' he asks.

'I don't know,' says Frank. Sirens rang out like church bells. The skyline danced with fire. He can't remember the gestures. 'Pretty hard?'

'If you hadn't picked up that hammer,' says Jackson, backlit by the window and the water's leaden sway, 'we wouldn't be here.'

'If I hadn't picked up the hammer,' says Frank, 'you'd be dead.'

'Are you fucking mad?'

'That's what I thought – okay? What the fuck was I meant to do? Just stand there and watch him strangle you? He was killing you – that's what I saw – that's what I *thought* I saw – that you were dying.'

He arrived at the boat and saw a man atop Jackson, crushing the life from his brother's throat. What happened next happened so quickly and so fluently that it had felt, in the moment, like nothing at all, like breath. It hadn't felt wrong. He didn't hesitate. He'd lifted the hammer, lifted again.

Jackson stares at the window, Frank at the floor: pointless surfaces on which to rest their gaze whilst they quiver with hate for each other. The silence that swells between them has a physical texture. It curdles the air.

'What would you have done if it was me?' Frank asks. 'If I was lying there, dying there, with someone's hands on my throat? You wouldn't have done it, is that what you're saying? You'd have just, I don't know... *Watched*?'

'No – I was saying—'

'Why is this even an issue?' Frank snaps. 'The man gets paid to rob sofas off people who can't afford to eat. *He's* the reason we're here. I thought I was saving your life.'

'I wouldn't just have *stood* there and watched,' says Jackson. He kicks a shard of dinner plate, which ricochets off the wall. 'But I wouldn't have tried to murder him for no reason. That's what I'm saying.'

Tangled up in bickering, the brothers half forget the man. He is no longer the hulking beast he was last night. He is shrunken, tied-up, prostrate, damp. He has the look of a gravely ill child.

Exhaustion enhances the alcohol. A giddy sense of unreality trembles at the edges of things. Instead of splashing water on the man's face, Frank holds the mug to his mouth.

'Drink,' he says.

Water pours through the man's teeth and over his tongue. It pools in his throat and spills from his lips.

'He's not swallowing,' says Frank. 'He needs to drink.'

'I felt a pulse. His heart's beating.'

Frank slaps the man on the cheeks. No response. He tries again, harder. Harder. He pinches, he prods. Same story.

'I don't get it...' Frank begins. 'He's alive. Technically. But...'

Jackson shrugs. He digs a tobacco pouch out of his pocket. 'I'm not a doctor,' he says.

'He needs one,' says Frank. 'Like, immediately.'

'I know.'

Frank leans forward, his nose almost touching the man's. He pulls back an eyelid and looks into the flat-brown retina. The pupil is swollen, dark.

Frank yells at the top of his lungs.

'WAKE UP.'

Nothing. Feels like shouting at a doll. Facts flash through his head. You must keep a person awake after a bad concussion, otherwise – what? There are more neurons in the human brain than there are stars in the sky. In the city that's fucking obvious: you can't see stars at all.

'WAKE UP. WAKE UP.'

A drop of Frank's spittle glistens against the man's cheek. He wipes it off with the hem of his jumper. Having done so, he licks his finger. A stubborn slick of dried blood clings to the man's temple. Frank works at the mark with the thumb of his right hand, cradling the skull with his left, until the mark is gone.

'I'M SORRY I KILLED YOU,' Frank shouts.

'He can't hear you,' Jackson says.

He holds the lighter's flame to the ragged tip of his rollie. Inhales. Exhales. Smoke swims through the room. He rests his head against the wall and shuts his eyes.

Frank squats on his haunches, hugging his knees. 'He's not waking up,' he says. 'It's not like a computer, is it? You can't just turn a person off and on.'

'Jesus,' Jackson says. 'I said leave it.'

'How? He's not going to disappear, is he?'

'Frank – you're not thinking, you're just saying words. Think for one second, alright? *Think*.'

'I think all the fucking time!' Frank yells. 'I just think the wrong things.'

Sea wind ruffles the reed-beds. Pebbles chatter as they turn in the waves. Even out here, in this tidal emptiness, the brothers hear a far-off crackle as the city warms to life.

'We should call an ambulance,' says Frank. 'He's probably bleeding in there. It looks bad. I feel bad. We could leave him on the path and call them later, when we're far enough away.'

'We'll never be far enough away,' says Jackson.

'What do you mean?'

Jackson stares at the floor.

Frank shuts his eyes for a moment. Visualising stuff helps him think. The image that comes to mind is of a mountain stream. The water's so clear he can see the bottom, dark fish flexing in the shallows, sunlight playing on the stones.

He opens his eyes.

'Let's kill him then,' he says. 'Properly this time.'

'How?'

'I don't know. I could hit him, then at least we'd know he's dead for real.'

Jackson almost laughs. 'Maybe you're right,' he says. 'I don't know. We had a plan before, didn't we?'

'We were heading out to sea, but I'm not sure—'

Jackson shakes his head, narrows his eyes, and stubs his cigarette out on the wall.

'We should never have stopped,' he sighs. His eyes look hollow, drained. 'Get up. Let's go.'

The buoy is joyful. Frank watches it dance, slapped about by playful waves. A beard of ragged seaweed flails beneath its tangerine scalp. It leaps up, splashes under, lollops sideways, flops on its face.

'Don't know why you're laughing,' Jackson says. He scans the horizon. The wind makes a rasping noise as it buffets his hood. Light rain sparkles in the air.

'The buoy,' says Frank.

'What about it?'

'Look at it go!'

The brothers have sailed as far out as they dare. Apart from the rainclouds and the endlessly trafficking aeroplanes, the sky is clear. Wind turbines bristle nearby. Further off is a pair of container ships, monolithic and grey.

'I guess this is it,' says Frank.

Jackson nods but says nothing.

The army's tidal islands are the closest part of land: long, low strips of mud patterned silver and black, like mackerel. Red signal lights warn ships to steer clear.

'You sure we're doing the right thing?' Frank asks.

'Not really,' Jackson replies. 'We have to do something, though. We can't just...'

'I know, but...'

'It's better this way.'

They've laid the man out at the rear of the boat, near the rusted red hatch where the engine lurks.

'He's not going to wake up, is he?' Frank asks. 'He's, what do they call it...'

Out in the open, exposed to air and rain, the man's cheeks have begun to blush.

Jackson frowns. 'He's gone,' he says. 'We tried everything. Even if we got him to hospital right now...'

'It would be too late?'

'You don't come back from something like that.'

Frank watches the man's eyeballs, which seem to shift, like a dreamer's, beneath their lids: light playing over the skin in the prickling rain.

'We would have had to get him help last night, like straight away,' he says.

'And we didn't.'

'We couldn't.'

The company's logo is embroidered on the boiler suit's breast pocket, near the man's heart. A red circle. Inside it is an armoured knight, mounted, clutching a jousting stick, with a St George's flag on his shield. The

171

brothers see the logo all over the city. On hoardings, building sites, offices, uniforms, locked doors.

'He's one of them,' says Frank.

Jackson nods. 'They would have made an example of us,' he says. 'You saw what they were doing to the others. They had vans full of them, all tied up. Truncheons. Water cannons. You know how they'll spin it.'

Last night is a blur of violence, panic, fire.

'It doesn't feel right,' he says. 'He's a person.'

'You've done it already.'

'I didn't have a choice, it was him or you. What about family? He might have kids.'

'You can't think about that. You can't let thoughts like that in your head.'

'But it's already in there.'

Frank watches the orange buoy lollop and dance. It no longer looks funny and free, but mocking.

'Listen,' Jackson says. 'There's no good way. There's just really, really bad, and then there's something worse than that. Those are the options. That's it.'

The man is wrapped up in blue ropes. Earlier, Frank carried armfuls of heavy objects from the boat and onto the roof. Frying pans. A metal stool. Two crowbars. A full can of gloss. Tins of soup, ravioli, beans. The unwieldy weights are knotted and cinched at points all over the man: arms, torso, waist, feet, neck.

'He looks like a charm bracelet,' says Frank. 'Will it work?'

'Maybe. I guess he'll sink for a bit and then...'

'The tide?'

Jackson shrugs. 'We'll be gone by then. Or caught. Either way...'

Frank pictures the body's descent through the water. Shapes emerge from the murk: archipelagos of sunken stone, forests of swaying seaweed, the sandy blankness of the ocean floor.

'Ready?' Jackson asks.

Frank nods. 'We should say something first.'

'Like what?'

'I don't know. An apology? A prayer?'

'This isn't a funeral. We don't even know the guy.'

'But—'

'Do it,' Jackson snaps. 'The sooner you do it, the sooner we go.'

Frank tightens his grip on the hammer. It has begun to feel like an extension of his body, a familiar, almost comforting weight. He lifts it high above his head and readies his body to strike.

He has decided to aim for the temple, the weakest spot in the skull. One swift, hard blow to end it, finally. Then, as he's about to strike, Frank's muscles seize up. A sick feeling blooms in his stomach. Raindrops crackle at his ears.

'Jackson,' he hisses, pointing.

But his brother has seen it already: the man's open eyes.

VI. THE WHITE BIRD

I had the drowning dream again. I had it for years as a child, once a week at least, and it has recently returned. In the dream, our mother appears as a shadowed swimmer, a kind of mermaid. The long green water is body-warm and I'm surrounded by music. Sunlight plays on the ocean's surface, a second sky, as sunken bells toll in the valley below.

My phone's alarm is screaming, drilling noise into the tender core of my head.

I hit Snooze. Turn over. Sink my face in the pillow's protection.

    The wall can wait
   despite what he says
because the bedding's still warm
with the imprint of
 heat from
  my sleep
  and
  Alarm! Drilling my brainstem.
  I thumb Off

and push back the bedding. My limbs greet the morning chill. It is bright outside but the sky is restless, clouds scudded white on the blue, and in the dimness of the waking room I feel the chill of a cold day approaching.

Sit up. Lean forward. Observe.

    6.42am

Well.

I stand in my boxers on the carpet's fuzz and squint through my sleep at the world. A melody loops in my head, a catchy constellation of fading notes, half-remembered from the dream.

I peer through the window at the yard and the field.

I breathe on the pane and draw an eye on the condensation.

The windows are single-glazed, the frames warped in their casings. But the view of sloping streets, the slanted field, and the glancing curve of the river through a lattice of trees will sometimes floor me.

In my room, with its cod-Victorian metal-framed bed, and its gloomy vine-patterned wallpaper, I have two luxuries. One is the window, which bathes me in view; the other's the sink, in which I bathe myself.

There is a mirror above the sink, spattered with globs of toothpaste and soap-froth, and in its grubby doubling I wince at my morning face, that manic glint in my eyes. I hover in the mirror like a ghoul.

Soon the sink is filled.

I dunk my face in the brief lucid shock of the water and hold my breath.

Eyes open.

Porcelain-white like an acre of snow.

Somewhere I read that putting your face below water like this triggers the diving response in your body, which slows your heart and brings calm to your functions. There have been times when I have needed this influence, when it felt like my heart would burst. The water brings me back to my pulse. In that process of returning, I remember two things: my body is living; another has drowned.

The comparison calms me. I don't know why.

Lean back. Dry my face with the scratchy towel.

I love the parched nature of this old washed thing, the thirst with which its fibres guzzle water off my cheeks. I brush my teeth and, scrubbing, foamy-mouthed, the window catches me again. I see the crispness of the light outside, the edges of everything sharp.

I remember my mission and quickly get dressed.

The drystone wall disintegrated. It happened last week when the river burst. In the mornings I stood at this window and watched the flooded field. The waters were clear and flat. Shadows moved through the sunken grass. The stones of the drystone grew buoyant.

When the river went back to normal, the lawn was scattered with crazy paving, no barrier left between the land and the path.

Dressed in jeans, boots, T-shirt, and jacket, I creep down creaking stairs and into the kitchen, the slanted light cool on the night-cooled floor. It feels like the world is sleeping. Like time just stopped.

If time has stopped I have time for a coffee.

I fill a saucepan, set it on the hotplate, and wait for the water to seethe.

Funny how brains behave when half asleep.

Warped memories and dream-dregs slosh in the skull.

I see:

myself on Leonard's balcony with Jackson, chucking planes at warm winds/a city alight in a torrent of rain, asters circling as lightning flares/our landscape from above, wooded in places, rusted in others, slashed with suburban grey/a long, winding river inscribed in the land, leading out to sea/a crimson wound in a crushed skull/a jungle asleep under stars.

The water boils and I make the coffee, black and strong, two sugars, stirring the granules and watching them foam and dissolve on the steaming whirlpool.

I could drink it in this kitchen, domestic implements for company. But there is work to do, before more work.

I step outside.

The woods that surround our town are turning green.

February.

Winter should be its most tenacious, but spring, it seems, is here.

Listen... That murmuring rumour of growth in the soil. The street's far end is shot with yellow, daffodils defying the cold soil, cute fuck-yous to the fading frost.

The paved street crackles under my boots as I walk.

Sunshine thumps through blue pools in the clouds overhead, smacking the slate roofs, making them hum with light. The blissful weather makes me urge for nicotine.

I pat my pockets. No tobacco.

Oh well.

Left at the corner, I head for the square which is really a circle: the empty core of the old town's concentric design.

There is an object here which I sit on sometimes, an upturned barrow with gnarled old wheels. I sit and scratch my head and inhale the herbal fragrance of rained-on grass and watch the droop-headed daffodils nod in the breeze.

I have a problem with the news. I check it compulsively, reflexively, without really knowing why. It's a habit that brings me nothing but low-level stress and fragmented distraction – for once, I won't do it.

For a few minutes, sipping coffee, I consider sending Jackson a pic of my boots or the morning sky. When he wakes up later this morning, he will see the photograph and notice the time-stamp and think, with a twinge of jealous pride:

Frank was awake before me?

I don't send the photo. Instead, I watch an aeroplane crawl through the sky and wonder how many messages, how many billions of bytes, are being transmitted right now through the upper atmosphere where the oxygen thins and the signals fly quicker.

Our phones were dead when we arrived. We didn't know if we'd found the right place. It was a warren of crooked shells. Half the roofs had collapsed. The floors were overgrown with tangled bushes, moss-carpets, flourishing vines.

The rusted pipes gave nothing. The sockets were cold.

We stood in a tumbledown kitchen and laughed.

For months, it was Jackson and I and the buildings. Hiding out because we had to, scratching nourishment from the woods.

We lived off huge alien mushrooms and bitter leaves. We slaked our thirst at the brownish river, hoping it wasn't poisoned, swimming with cowshit: we couldn't complain.

We'd arrived, after all.

Survived.

We weren't locked up, or dead, or worse.

(There is worse.)

In a strange way, we had what we wanted.

In a sense, we were free.

So even in the midst of the hunger, the itching filth, the panic that kept us awake if the night-foxes didn't, in the midst of a chronic discomfort we'd brought upon ourselves, there was a kernel of silvery something – call it relief.

The city was sinking. That much was clear. The slush-corrupted, tidal earth was slowly guzzling the buried foundations, gnawing the paving, chewing the streets.

'I guess that's why everyone left,' I said, 'all those years ago? Basements filled with water. Sofas floating out the door.'

Jackson nodded: '*Hmmmmmmmh.*'

He knew a few facts.

At first it was a rumour he couldn't qualify, having never been here. A tale he'd heard somewhere, mentioned once or twice in the Citadel, about a town that had been abandoned, the streets lined with empty rooms.

They'd poured the concrete into trenches dug deep in the earth but the earth was soaking. It was riddled with hair's-breadth waterways and stagnating pools. Amphibians luxuriated. Pond-weed skimmed the puddles. The river (we learned the hard way) flooded every spring.

I stand and cross the square to the fountain in the centre, a stone basin, unadorned. The windows of buildings opposite are dark, the others not yet awake.

Strange I can say that. The others. The friends, if that's the word, with whom we live.

It wasn't always the aim.

We went on walks to get a grip on the neighbourhood. The steel-works was a cathedral of rust. The houses were biscuits left out in the rain. The viaducts were highways of rubble and moss. We cycled down them. Ripples rang out as we crossed the puddles.

Months before arriving, we found some pictures of the place on our phones. They were film stock, black-and-white. I'd seen the diagrams, the architects' schemes: colour-coded circles that intersected like atoms in molecules, Venn diagrams of idealised living.

A garden city.

That was the phrase.

I pictured a street lined with palm trees and dotted with towers of sunstruck gold, where lushness flourished in the gaps between sandstone palaces. I saw dirigibles sailing high over the glinting spires of ancient industry, a palace on a hill with steep steps all around.

Instead we got this dinner plate dropped on a marsh. Brick follies slowly sinking into mud beneath our boots, so wet you could practically swim in it. Unfinished roads thrusted like piers into grassy nothing, infrastructure patiently waiting for houses that never arrived.

On the far side of the cobbled square, the stones of which have been nudged loose by insistent grass, is the old Town Hall.

It's my favourite part, right here, where the houses peter off and the main road slopes towards the factory brazen in morning sun. At the road's end are the camouflage colours of the muddy grass, and, beyond that, the glint of the river.

The water flashes like a turning knife.

For a while I watch it stream.

Right there, beside the willow, is the patch of riverbank on which we landed.

I thought, back then, we were going to die.

Maybe starve. Maybe drown.

Most likely we'd be woken one morning by a knock on the door, and blackvests, lifters, or just a few men, would storm into our room and beat us.

I couldn't eat. Jackson had slept so little his eyes were as wild as a trapped fox's, scrabbling round the cage of our slow-moving barge.

We sailed for days and nights / moved through towns and fields / slept under stars / ate bitter berries / ducked from headlights / ran from bulls.

We smiled at strangers on the waterways as if nothing at all was wrong. And then, after months, we arrived.

Unknown river. Strange trees.

No one anywhere.

Us.

I remember the feverish mood of the journey. Convinced we were being followed, I conjured spirits in every shadow, heard the madness of the chattering worms, and told myself the clouds were spacecraft, the sun a vast pitiless eye.

Every night, after mooring the boat, we would strike off into the fenlands, marshes, or fields beneath the crackling pylons. If there were woods nearby we would lose ourselves, lugging a two-man tent and a box of matches.

We foraged and stole our food.

Woody clumps of samphire burned our lips with salt.

I tightened my trousers with lengths of rope and swallowed pints of water for lunch.

Once I caught a rabbit, almost by accident. It was resting in a glade and I struck it. In the light of a sputtering fire, we began to skin the rabbit, fingers slick with its slippery, pastel guts. But the muscles beneath the fur were such a glossy, naked pink, so eerily like a newborn child's, we couldn't bring ourselves to eat it.

We spent about a year like that, patching up the old boat as best we could, losing our minds in that airless cabin, guided by fireflies and satellites, steering clear of the urban lights.

Things had begun to settle down, after the madness of the eviction, after that summer of riots.

But that was out there, in the country.

Our world was in here, on the boat.

Night in the woods had a feeling, one that cities hide us from: a daily dying of the world you only feel if you're out in the middle of nowhere, surrounded by the skeletal shapes of ancient trees and the rustle of life in the undergrowth. The darkness creeps inside you. It taints your blood and stains your bones.

At night, the world died around us.

Every morning, it woke again.

The dawn was a pale blue medicine that soaked through a gauze of branches, tugging me out from shivering not-quite-sleep. It is dawn right now and I'm attuned to the music of water beyond the houses. Elastic shadows stretch across the street as I head for the river, ready to snap and vanish as the sun ascends.

The factory looms above the rooftops, tangled,

grand, and castle-grey.

When Jackson told me he knew an empty town, I didn't believe him. Sounded like bullshit to me. But then we travelled along the river

through the city's lights

past the ship yards and docks where the river twists inland and the city gives way to suburb

the suburb gives way to trees

the trees gather in woods that brood

on low hills and flood

the valleys

and there it was:

the dead place we'd come to revive.

A mad industrialist built it sometime last century, Jackson said. The plan was to revolutionise manufacture but the whole thing flopped. He was trying too hard to be opposites, I guessed: a filthy-rich utopian.

There were factories, a steel works, workers' houses – a boom town, all of it shut down now.

The company busted and jobs dried up.

Since then it had been left to grow wild, coloured by spray-paint murals and darkened by scars of arson, but otherwise empty. If this had happened in the capital, our city of birth, the land would have been flattened decades ago and turned into a Bad Thing (as we saw it then) stuffed with luxury flats for numbskull squillionaires in cahoots with the Powers that Be, the Powers who'd scorned us, the Powers we loathed – opinions that make me cringe so hard today it feels like my face will implode.

I drift into the terraces, neat lines of near-identical two-up-two-downs. They look like copy-pasted jpegs.

This is where Jackson lives.

For a while we lived together under the same roof, partly out of fear – we thought we'd be busted in the early hours, like the night of eviction. But we drove each other nuts, and in time our shouting came to blows. So, for the last five years, we've kept a distance.

His house isn't quite en-route, so I take a detour.

Squinting at the light streaming down from the sky, inhaling air that smells of coldness and silt from the river, I reach a front garden. An enamel bathtub is filled with rainwater. It wasn't there the last time I passed. The soupy water is flecked with fallen leaves that pool around stone gnomes and clay pots filled with plastic roses.

Something tickles the back of my brain
like a waterweed brushing my foot as I swim.

It takes a while before I nail it: the Citadel's front yard had a similar bath, and in the bath were plastic gnomes.

Jackson's curtains are drawn.

For once I'm the early riser, the go-getter, and when I return triumphant to the yard, steaming with effort and strength, my face a little sun-brushed, my arms muscled and bulging and glossed with sweat, he will see that I've returned – his younger brother, his weaker other – and he will say:

'Frank, by golly, you've fixed the wall!'

And I shall reply:

'Yes, brother Jackson, I did so. Witness the birth of a new beginning.'

The road's end. Another detour, to the factory this time. Ivy crawls over its outer walls. Ladders glimmer in the sliding light.

I pause.

Someone is watching.

I turn and scan the grass and the buildings' windows, squinting across the dark panes. I think, perhaps, Jackson has followed. I wait for a while and watch.

My brother used to tell me that we'd never have a home unless we built it for ourselves. He wanted me to know that the world wasn't easy, life was a grind. Getting dirty, being bruised, wrecked, ruined, broken by the world, were part of his bloody mind-set. He had a lot of rage back then (still does) but it was channelled in peculiar ways.

Most of the time, he worked his anger out through me.

I was a lightning rod, a punch-bag, a piece of clay.

I was his project, his burden, his brother.

And in his odd, awkward way I guess that's what he meant by 'a city inside us'.

He did mean an actual place, a physical structure, a solid version of those buildings he forced me to draw when we lived in the city. But more than that (I think) he wanted family.

A seagull swings into view, riding currents of air.

I can't see Jackson or anyone else. So I continue my trudge to the factory, haunted by the sense of being watched, convincing myself it was just the white bird.

The factory is out of bounds. But no one obeys the rules, least of all me. The side-door creaks as I slip inside.

The cushioned smell of moss and the hush of the
building;
    dust-motes thickened to mortar
    in columns of solid sun.

For a while, I thought that Jackson and I could live
in here. We would build four-poster beds in giant spaces
and live like kings. I wandered through the rooms with
my brother, astonished. Wild stuff had crept inside. The
floors had bred carpets of earth.

        Vines darkened the windows, thick webs like
optical nerves.

Pigeons thronged the distant eaves, foxes padded
through blast furnaces and rolling mills, mice scuttled
down huge ceramic vats and spindly conveyor belts.

    Trees grew slantwise in the mortar.

In one of the rooms, where a huge furnace stood
like an oversized human heart, bulging with veins of
chrome, a hole in the roof allowed sunlight to pierce the
gloom, and in this pool of light a twisted, hard-leafed
shrub had grown.

        I kick a rusted bolt and watch it skitter: a dotted
line dashed through the dust.

Some nights, if the weather's bad, we will gather here,
after dark, and drink, smoke, talk. Groups of us, ten or
twenty. We might cook food. Someone might strum a
guitar (I wish they wouldn't). Someone might carry
their laptop in, and we'll watch something on the screen.

Jackson once said that two people could make a
society. The way we were with each other, the way we be-
haved, could set the conditions for it. Now we have more
than two. We have a town of strangers who've since
become friends, people from the cities and suburbs or
further afield.

I head back outside, squinting.

For days last week, the water was high but not yet muddy. You could see the grass sway in it like green hair. I ran down in the afternoon like an idiot, wearing nothing but underwear, and dove headfirst.

Now I head down the sloping grass towards the wall.

I'm not yet thirty – I'm no old man – but the morning keeps bringing me back, and now I see a night, many years ago now, which I've tried my best to bury.

We didn't know what to do. We tried to wake the man but he was dead, we couldn't wait. Asters circled overhead, the blackvest trucks were parked nearby: it would be minutes before they found us.

Jackson turned the key. The boat throbbed to life. I gripped the hammer – I couldn't let go – as the boat slid along the canal.

The man lay sprawled at my feet like a rag doll, leaking blood on a crumpled rug. Through the windows I couldn't see much, just water as we moved.

I tied the man's wrists with duct tape and joined my brother in the wheelhouse. He didn't say a word; he didn't ask about the man; we stood in the tense wooden box, and the strangest thing happened.

It had not happened before that point. It has not happened since.

I felt his thoughts and he felt mine. We didn't speak: we didn't have to.

As the boat swung slowly round the bends in the branching canal and the buildings loomed dark and tall as cliffs we knew that any one of those broken windows could be hiding eyes, and that the skies were adrift with asters combing the ground with their lights.

In our panicked frame of mind we made a false equivalence: that if we were caught we might as well have been killed, because our lives would be over.

The boat swung round the canal's last bend and we saw through the rain-spat windshield the river galloping past, lit by the firefly bulbs of the apartment buildings on the far banks, with the towers to the west and the sky-scrapers to the east.

We entered the river's flow and I slipped outside.

On the deck, in pummelling rain, I crept down the boat as it swayed on the river and gripped the skylight to steady myself. Beyond the clustered anonymous apartment complexes, past the building sites and ruined wharves, I caught a glimpse of the flicker of dying flames and the spotlights pointed down and the smoke leaking skyward, a tower of vapour.

I saw no eyes. I heard no sirens.

Instead I saw, further upriver, a clutch of boats and a crosshatch of bridges. The river thinned to a heart of light; downriver, the riverbanks widened into darkness. And even though it was the wrong direction, I told my brother to go that way – to strike out from the city.

Jackson nodded because he knew. He was already turning the wheel.

I check the damage to the drystone wall. I pull the gloves on and get to work, knees creaking as I duck and lift the stones.

Every stone is a different shape, has a different weight. Some are perfect rectangles, all sharp edges and clean lines; others are broken shards and flints, like you might find on a primitive weapon, or lodged in a cave-man's collarbone. A drystone wall is like a jigsaw. You fit the pieces back together until it's fixed.

I get started.

The barge was a small, slow vessel. Its engine hummed and throbbed, a senile putter, no urgency, maddeningly slow. The far banks dribbled past. We were overtaken by other, faster vessels that shed expanding Vs of wake and made our barge sway as we moved.

Soon we were under the financial towers rising miles into the sky like crystal cliffs, the air around them radiated with turquoise light. At their tops they gave off gusts of white smoke, red lights flashing to warn off planes.

We sailed on.

The boat in its highest gear.

But still we dawdled, pottered, dragged our wet heels through the water as the sky began to brighten overhead and the banks on either side resolved to vague forms, a wall of shadow becoming distance becoming beach.

I think we'd lost our minds by that point. But we tried to bury our burden.

Black sand under our fingernails.

Grit of crustacean shells.

We travelled across the estuary in the pale dawn, bone-tired, Jackson at the wheel. I gripped the rungs on the front of the boat squinting into the rain and the cold stinging air.

I went back down into the boat, not knowing what else to do, and squatted and peered at the lifter's face. It was like a joke-shop zombie mask, lifeless rubber, but his eyes were spinning beneath closed lids.

My instinct was to hit him.

To kill him properly and for good.

This dead man, now alive, or half alive, was possibly brain-dead; at minimum, very badly concussed. I did the only thing I could have done. I called my brother.

Daylight on the river. Across the estuary we saw the enormous commercial ports with their red-blue-yellow containers stacked like toys.

Further out, wind turbines stood like mechanical

daffodils, slow blades keeping time in the ocean's distance. The boat chugged petrol and we steered a slow course back in the direction we'd sailed from, back to land.

One option.

We came to a shuddering halt beside a wharf on the northern bank. Near was a boatworks with skippers, trawlers, lasers, longboats in the driveway. The lifter was almost awake, baby-talking, stringing half-words together as I wrapped a strip of fabric round his eyes (he'd seen us already – we hoped he'd forget).

Together we lugged him ashore for the second time that morning.

I thought that maybe we were trapped in an infinite loop: purgatory. He could stagger, just about, with us for balance as he stumbled, us caked in sand. We slumped up a ramp and down a sideroad.

An alcove between two buildings; a shadowed lee in which to hide.

Both our phones were dead so Jackson emptied his wallet, found two silver coins, and ran off for a payphone, if payphones still existed, we didn't know. And then it was me and him, the man I'd almost killed.

He was groaning, his head to one side. I felt sorry for him then – for the first time ever, actually. He looked like a fever-sick kid.

Motherless, lost.

I saw myself as Jackson once described me. Sitting on a rock, happy, laughing, knowing nothing as we walked through a valley in punishing sun.

The man was pawing at the blindfold, breathing deep erratic breaths, and so I told him to stop. He wasn't blind, he'd had an accident, that's all.

I teased his hands away.

At first it was babble-snatches.

Later, half-formed words emerged.

He asked me where he was and what had happened.

I think that's what he asked, anyway; the words turned to mush in his mouth. I told him he'd tripped and banged his head, fallen into the river, and help was on its way.

Jackson appeared at the end of the road. I put a finger to my lips; my brother whispered he'd made the call and he told me to leave. I lingered. The man was drifting in and out of consciousness, writhing in delirious pain. I found it hard to leave him

but Jackson tugged my arm again: he hadn't told me to leave but to *lift*.

We needed to dunk the man. Get rid of our fingerprints, skin cells, hair, the fibres of our clothes – any microscopic, miniscule thing that could connect us to him.

So we carried the mumbling man to the cold brown water. We unzipped the grey boiler suit, tugged it off his arms, torso, legs, and waist. He lay there naked in the dawn. His skin was as pale as candlewax; he was tugging at his blindfold like a nervous dog. We dunked his body in the slosh –

the strangest thing happened.

His body went limp. His muscles relaxed.

An almost-smile dawned on his face.

We lowered his head after that, performing what must have looked from afar like a baptism. Then we dragged him onto shore, jumped aboard the boat, and sailed away.

After that, we checked the news repeatedly. We googled:

man killed estuary

missing killers
jackson frank
citadel murder
coma lifter
missing suspects citadel assault

We even set up email alerts. But nothing, no news.

A year and a half after arriving here, once we had finally convinced each other that we hadn't been tracked, we went to a payphone in a nearby town, in hats and scarves to hide our faces, and stood together in the plastic box as the rain poured around us and the bright yellow trams rattled past.

Jackson dialled Nell's mobile. We weren't sure she would answer, or if she even had the same number. Then her voice came on the line, croaky, distant, still familiar.

She was surprised, relieved, to hear from us. No one knew what had happened, where we'd gone. She asked us where we were. We didn't tell her, didn't know how far the word would spread.

She hadn't heard about a lifter.

Actually no, she said, she *had* heard something, actually – but it was one among many – the eviction had been carnage, historic for all the wrong reasons. Hijacked. Corrupted.

They hadn't been able to identify anyone. And yes, the blackvests asked her who it might have been, but no, she hadn't told them.

Caspar hadn't been so lucky. He'd gone to court with bloody stitches like a zip down the side of his head and would be in jail, it seemed, for a very long time.

Lali had also been arrested. Suspended sentence. We asked about Arthur. The line went quiet.

'You haven't heard?'

Arthur died that night.

It must have happened shortly after we left. Towards the end of the eviction, he rampaged around the Citadel's empty rooms, setting light to mattresses, furniture, sheets: a blaze of glory (he'd have thought).

When they finally caught him, collapsed in the smoke of the blaze, he was lucid. Then, while they drove him away, he slumped.

Jackson went quiet.

We asked Nell what she was doing. We said she should come and live with us in the new place, our garden city. We would find somewhere for her to work; she could use the steel works as a studio. She said she'd think about it. We said goodbye. Swapped numbers. Lost contact over time. It's been about a year since we spoke.

Once half the wall is fixed, I decide I've done enough.

I'm not being lazy, I never shirk. I think the wall looks better with a gap.

Here, though, we are surrounded by wilderness, beyond which lies a suburb, beyond which lies a city that barely knows we exist. We get visitors sometimes, boys who come to gawp and taunt on mini motorbikes and BMXs, new arrivals who've heard about us online, journalists sometimes, photographers, dog-walkers, wild-walkers, weirdos.

The stones are stacked. The wall is finished.

I wander towards the river, over shaggy grass dotted with flowers, in the direction of trees around which bracelets of drooping bluebells grow.

The steel works cast a long and complex shadow over the waters and the grass. Turning, I see the field slope up to the brick houses and streets, and, beyond it, the main road leading into haze. Soon I will go back there, knock on Jackson's door, and we will sit down in the kitchen, drink two mugs of bitter coffee, and plan the day. I feel a pang of boredom at the thought. All this grass, this abundance of untainted air, leaves me longing for the grotty solid stuff of concrete and tarmac and clay, the itching of pollution in the air.

I walk to the water's edge and dip my hands into the rushing water. Kneeling, I take a sip (ferrous, gum-achingly cold) and scoop handfuls of it over my head.

My mind drifts back to the time my brother took me to that building site. It wasn't the first one, nor the last, but it sticks in my mind like a shard of bottle-glass in river mud, catching the light. It was summer. The city was melting. I think June. Heat was trapped in the smog and pollen, the dusty paving stones and gluey tarmac. Everyone sweating.

No one at work.

Topless men with football shirts tucked into the waistbands of shorts slouched down roasting streets with cans of lukewarm lager. Kids with sticky lollies stood squinting on street corners. Blood-heat, fighting heat, fucking heat.

We jumped a fence and ran along a gully past dig-gers until we reached a curved building shaped like a horseshoe, an old estate that shielded us from view. Half the building had been demolished; the other half would follow soon.

Hot chunks stood in a jagged heap with thick dust floating off them.

The debris was studded with jutting metal and glass and in places I spotted crushed sofas, smashed fridges, broken mirrors, broken window frames – a blitzed heap of a ruined building, a tangle of broken homes.

Jackson tied a bed sheet round my neck, swimming goggles over my eyes. I was a comic-book hero, a dirty city Superboy, cape afloat behind me as I climbed.

My brother had begun to teach me about the world and our place within it, how we lived in the shadows, unwanted, unseen. We were kids who came from nothing, were nothing. The city would only make room for us if we forced it to, the way you force a door with a crowbar, or use plumber's freeze to smash a lock:

these little acts were ways of opening space to breathe in a city that didn't want us, wouldn't protect us, narrowed choices to a flatline.

That afternoon, a Sunday I think, the building site a burning basin of heat and light, we summoned a kingdom of dust. It lasted a couple of hours, but in those hours we were electric.

I began to understand

or maybe just feel

a sense of freedom on the rubble's peak,
white dust-spires swaying like serpents around me,

my hands on my hips and the sun in my eyes and a thick taste of dust in my mouth.

I squinted down the mountain at the chunk of shadow in which my brother stood.

It must have been an illusion: the city disappeared.

All I could see was Jackson, the patch of ground he stood on, like an island in empty space. I lifted my hand and waved at him, screamed at him to join me, watched him clamber up the concrete and into the heat of the sun.

Acknowledgements

Thanks to: Jacques Testard, for guidance, insight, and support, without which this book would not exist; Alice Hattrick, for invaluable conversations about structure and tone – much of what's best in this book is thanks to her; to Ray O'Meara, for his beautiful design; Ben Eastham and Matt Gold, who read the novel in early drafts and provided important feedback and much-needed encouragement; and Francesca Wade, for casting her precise eye across the final draft. I am grateful to Arts Council England, who provided a grant that enabled me to complete a first draft of the novel. I am also, as ever, grateful to my parents for their unflagging support, and to my sister, who helped me understand what it means to be a brother.

Fitzcarraldo Editions
243 Knightsbridge
London, SW7 1DN
United Kingdom

ISBN 978-1910695-51-7

Design by Ray O'Meara
Typeset in Fitzcarraldo
Printed and bound by TJ International

fitzcarraldoeditions.com

Fitzcarraldo Editions